WHITE FANG II:

MYTH OF THE WHITE WOLF

WHITE FANG II:

MYTH OF THE WHITE WOLF

A Novel by Elizabeth Faucher
Based on the Motion Picture from Walt Disney Pictures
Co-Producer Justis Greene
Based on the Screenplay Written by David Fallon
Produced by Preston Fischer
Directed by Ken Olin

SCHOLASTIC INC.
New York Toronto London Auckland Sydney

ISBN 0-590-48611-X

12 11 10 9 8 7 6 5 4 3 2   4 5 6 7 8 9/9

Printed in the U.S.A.   01

First Scholastic printing, May 1994

WHITE FANG II:

MYTH OF THE WHITE WOLF

Chapter 1

It was spring, but the Alaska morning was still cold and foggy and bleak. The year was 1899, and the rugged wilderness looked as though no human being had ever set foot in it. The civilized world was so far away that it might as well have been on another planet.

The dawn sky was starting to brighten, and a swift feral form ran through the lifting fog. The animal raced silently through the forest, his powerful legs churning, a white wave of fur rising and falling in the wind.

It was a wolf, flitting in and out of the fog like a ghostly optical illusion, stalking his unseen prey. His name was White Fang and he was running with his ears back, his head low, enjoying the hunt.

Suddenly, a boy holding a rifle appeared out of the mist. His name was Henry Casey. He was about twenty years old, with a thin, pale face. His heavy clothes were well-worn, and it was obvious that he had been roughing it for a long time. An outsider would have assumed that he was stalking White Fang, but in fact, he was hunting *with* White Fang.

Rifle ready to fire, he blindly followed White Fang through the forest. He moved as carefully as he could, trying — like the wolf — to be quiet, focused, and alert. Ahead of him, White Fang once more disappeared into the mist and Henry stopped, waiting for him to show again.

Ranging off to one side, White Fang caught sight of an eighteen point buck nibbling at moss on the side of a tree. The wolf froze, cocking his muzzle up and sniffing the air. Then he changed direction and, with his stomach close to the ground, crawled soundlessly, moving around the unsuspecting deer.

In the meantime, Henry was still looking for his unseen friend. He peered up a nearby hill, his rifle pointing at the ground. He heard the pounding of hooves on the earth and spun around in time to see the huge deer running straight at him, with White Fang hot on his trail.

Henry hesitated, transfixed by the sight of the magnificent animal, and the pause cost him. Before he could raise his rifle and get off a wild shot, the deer charged past him and Henry had to dive out of the way to keep from being trampled. He watched from the ground as the deer thundered up the hill and out of sight.

White Fang chased it briefly, then came galloping back, looking at Henry with what appeared to be annoyance.

"Potatoes again tonight," Henry said wryly.

White Fang had no response, other than turning and trotting up the hill.

Henry sighed, climbed laboriously to his feet, and followed him. When he caught up, he grabbed the wolf's ear playfully, and White Fang bit into his pants at the ankle, tripping him up. Henry laughed, grabbing him as he fell, and they both rolled across the ground together, until they were covered with dirt and stray twigs.

Then, sensing something up ahead, White Fang scrambled to his feet and moved forward, growling low in his throat.

Knowing that this was serious, Henry got up, too, brushing himself off as he did so. "What is it, White Fang?" he asked softly.

The wolf took a few cautious steps, still growling, and then Henry saw a man in his late forties snooping around outside the cabin where he and White Fang lived. The man had dark unwashed hair and a body that was more wiry than thin. He walked bow-legged, as a cowboy might, but his shifty-eyed persona seemed much more like a horse thief than a cowboy out on the range.

Henry looked down at White Fang, impressed by his alertness, and then they both walked down the trail towards the cabin, watching the intruder every step of the way.

The man was still prowling around the cabin, trying to peer inside. Finally he knocked on the door, hard enough to make the hinges shake.

"Looking for something?" Henry asked, standing behind him.

The man's hand froze in mid-knock and he turned with a phony smile, exposing tobacco-stained teeth.

"Well, howdy, boy!" he said heartily.

Henry nodded stiffly, staying a safe distance away. He had a protective hand twisted in the thick fur of White Fang's ruff, the other hand still held his rifle.

Noticing the gun, the man raised his hands politely, but also strayed a few steps to the side, moving closer to his own rifle, which was strapped to *his* battered old pack. The pack lay on the ground in an untidy heap.

"Name's Halverson," the man said, with his wide, fake smile. "Lloyd Halverson. I hate the name, so you can call me what you like." At that, he chuckled loudly, waiting for Henry to join in.

Henry just stood there, unsmiling, as White Fang approached the stranger and sniffed at him suspiciously.

"Now, the wolf here I remember vividly," Halverson said, with another chuckle. He showed Henry his yellowed teeth.

"Don't think I know *you* though. Where's that other boy? What was his name?"

Henry shrugged, not wanting to give this man anything until he figured out exactly what it was that he wanted. "You tell me."

"Ah . . ." Halverson thought for a minute, "Jack. Yeah, Jack. Un, Conroy, right?"

Since that *was* right, Henry nodded.

"Yep," Halverson agreed cheerfully. "Always did have a head for names. For all the good it did me." He chuckled some more, enjoying his own wit.

Henry managed to force a smile. "Jack went back to San Francisco about a year ago this time."

Halverson digested that for a few seconds. "You his brother?" he asked.

Henry shook his head. "A friend," he said, without elaborating. "He left me in charge of the claim."

"Huh," Halverson said, and gave that some thought, too. "Yeah, Jack and I set a spell — what, two, three years ago when I passed through. I been west o' here." He gestured vaguely to one side. "Bellied-up least a dozen digs. And I ain't the only one. Whole *country's* been picked clean." He shook his head ruefully. "It's sad to see."

6

Henry couldn't think of a comment he felt like making, so he just shrugged.

"Me, I'm packin' it in," Halverson said, without even pausing. "Headin' into Dawson. It ain't no time to travel with that water comin' up," he gestured towards the river, "but I cain't wait no more."

Henry nodded. The river had been rising lately. As the winter snows melted in the warmer spring air the runoff had flowed down into the streams that fed the river, making it swell over the banks on either side. As a rule, only a fool would try to travel the waters when the conditions were like that.

"How about you?" Halverson asked, conversationally. "Any luck?"

"None," Henry said.

Halverson's eyes narrowed slightly, and he looked around the wooden clearing. "Up here by ya'self?"

Henry nodded.

"What's your name?" Halverson asked.

"Henry," Henry said reluctantly. "Henry Casey."

Halverson nodded, stretched his back, yawned widely, and then spit on the ground and kicked dirt over it. He grinned at

7

Henry, like they both knew the same secret.

"Well, Henry," he drawled, "how do I know you ain't killed that boy and just took over here?"

Henry jerked his rifle up, leveling it at Halverson. "Move on, mister," he said in a very grim voice.

"Whoa, son," Halverson said, lifting his hands defensively. "I'm leavin', I'm leavin'. . . . Just take it easy now, okay?" He scuttled over to his pack, and bent to lift it onto his shoulders.

The sudden movements startled White Fang, who lowered his head and growled.

"Get a hold o' him," Halverson said. His voice rose with terror as he backed away.

"He does what he wants," Henry said, sounding as calm as the man sounded nervous. "Just don't move real fast."

Halverson nodded, picking up his pack and moving with terrifying slowness as he passed between Henry and the wolf, and walked off down the trail.

Henry watched him until he was out of sight, his expression worried. He didn't know what the man was up to, but he had a feeling that it was nothing good.

Chapter 2

Later that day, Henry crouched outside his cabin, shaking his rocker box, which was a wooden box with a metal grate in the bottom that he used to knock the dirt and silt away from the debris he collected while prospecting for gold. He sifted the heap of "short ends" he had piled up — rocks and pebbles and various bits of wood — looking eagerly for the telltale nuggets and flakes that would ensure his future.

There was a fire burning in the primitive stone firepit next to him, and whatever was in the cast-iron pot hanging above it was boiling away merrily. He had put together a bland fish and potato stew, and as it began to boil over, Henry wiped the dirt and mud from his hands onto his pants. Then he lifted the pot, burning his hands as he removed it from the fire. He winced, dropped it, and blew on his fingers to cool them.

Once the pain had eased, he picked up a heavy old silver spoon and dished the stew onto two tins, dividing it into precisely equal portions.

White Fang, who had been watching all of this from the edge of the woods, came trotting over, his tail waving with anticipation.

"Just in time," Henry said, and put one of the tins down on the ground for White Fang. After that, he took his own plate and sat down to eat, using his hands and chewing loudly.

There was no question that White Fang had better table manners.

After dinner, Henry went into the cabin and back to work. Soon he was surrounded by a pile of dirt as he weighed and bagged the gold he had recovered that day. Finished, Henry grinned at White Fang, who was licking his chops.

"I know what you're thinking," Henry said.

White Fang looked at him without blinking.

"You're figuring out how to spend your share," Henry said, and laughed. "Am I right?"

White Fang just kept looking at him.

"Right," Henry said.

Using his hunting knife, he pried up a loosened floorboard and put the sack in the hollowed-out space where he had stored the rest of his stash. It had been back-breaking work over a long period of time, but he now had *thirty* moose-hide bags of gold in there. More accurately, he now had a small fortune.

Henry sat back on his heels, admiring the neat rows of bulging sacks.

"My little pals," he said softly, almost crooning. "There's too many of you here now. Just too many. Gotta get you to Dawson." Dawson was the nearest outpost, where all of the local trappers and prospectors would go to buy supplies, and trade in their pelts and gold in exchange for cash or fooodstuffs. "Gotta go *soon*."

Then he carefully replaced the board, adjusting the corners until it was impossible to tell that board from any of the others.

Even a person who *knew* where the gold was would have trouble finding it.

Outside, a figure crept from the shadows of the trees and worked his way around the back of the cabin. He was carrying a rifle in one hand, and a skinned rabbit in the other. A stick broke underneath his weight and he paused, listening intently, hoping that he hadn't given his presence away.

It was Halverson — and he had come to cause trouble.

Inside the cabin, White Fang snapped to attention, having heard the tiny sound. Seeing his reaction, Henry sat up, too, looking uneasy. White Fang walked stiff-legged to the window, the hair on his ruff and back rising. Then, without even a growl of warning, he leaped through the opening and disappeared outside.

Halverson, in the meantime, had set up a steel trap and was hanging the dead rabbit to a tree branch right above it. Once that was done, he crawled into the underbush to wait for the wolf to be drawn into his cruel ambush.

White Fang sniffed at the cool Alaska air, catching a whiff of the enticing smell of meat. He kept sniffing, then followed the tantalizing scent, looking for its source. Meat was very hard for him to resist.

Halverson saw the wolf coming towards the trap, and smiled, easing back the hammer on his rifle. He would get rid of the predator once and for all.

White Fang heard the little click and stopped dead in his tracks. Then, he changed direction and circled around the other way.

Halverson craned his neck to see where the wolf had gone. He was about to give up and come out from his hiding place when he felt hot lupine breath on the back of his neck. He swallowed hard, and turned to see White Fang crouched behind him, ready to spring.

Instantly, Halverson's eyes dilated with fear.

"Well, there you are," he said, with his voice an octave higher than usual.

Before he had a chance to spin and get

off a shot, White Fang was on him, his paws thumping against the man's chest and knocking him down onto the deadly trap. The steel jaws clamped shut on Halverson's backside and he leaped up, screaming. He ran, still screaming, with the trap hanging from his pants and White Fang chasing after him.

As Halverson came yelling around the corner of the cabin, he slammed right into an also-running Henry. They both fell. Henry was the first one to jump up and he pointed his rifle at Halverson, while White Fang snarled down at him.

"Git the trap off me, boy!" Halverson pleaded. "Or shoot me where I lie."

It was a hard choice.

"Don't tempt me," Henry said.

But, in the end, he helped Halverson unsnap the steel jaws, and then stepped back, holding the rifle on him as Halverson waddled in pain over to his pack. The man picked it up and limped into the woods, apparently beaten.

Once he was gone, Henry looked around, forced to make a decision he had been putting off.

"There'll be more coming through," he

said aloud. "I worked too hard to let them steal it from me now. Gotta get that gold to the bank." He looked over at White Fang. "What do you say we drag the raft out and float on into Dawson?"

White Fang cocked his head to one side, doing his best to understand every word.

"Besides, we need supplies," Henry said. "You up for it?"

White Fang's only response was to cock his head to the other side.

Henry nodded. "Okay, good. We'll leave in the morning." Then, excited by the prospect of a trip, he headed into the cabin to pack.

White Fang stayed right where he was, staring into the woods. He wanted to make sure that Halverson never even *considered* coming back.

If he did, White Fang was going to make him regret it.

Chapter 3

Miles down the swollen river, there was a small Haida Indian village. Despite its tiny size, it was active and full of life. A ceremony was in progress. There were drums pounding, whistles blowing, and voices chanting.

Along the riverbank, among a forest of intricately carved totem poles, sat the once-grand Haida Wolf House. The tribe had fallen on hard times, and the grandeur only the elders could still remember was long past. Today, times were tough, and survival was a constant struggle. But the tribe was determined, against all odds, that they would return to their former glory.

The Wolf House was the Haida Chief's family domicile and the center of the Indians' community life. Flanked by smaller dwellings constructed from rough-hewn wood, the Wolf House stood tall. It was more ornate than the others, with faded, but elaborate, paintings of wolves, killer whales, ravens, and frogs adorning the cedar-plank walls. Each of the paintings celebrated a Haida legend or tradition.

The Chief's son, Moses, and a young warrior named Peter carried the Chief's body gently out of the Wolf House, following the tribe's Holy Man in their traditional funeral ceremony procession. Kat'rin, one of the tribe's most beloved and respected women, and Moses' beautiful niece Lily came next, followed by the rest of the Haida villagers. A lone white man, a preacher from the town of Dawson, came out last, trailing behind the others, clutching his worn Bible.

Moses and Peter walked over to the casket, which had been hollowed out of a tree. It had a long pole attached to each side so that it could be carried. They set the body very respectfully inside the hollow log in a semireclining position, and then several other men stepped forward to help them

17

lift the cumbersome log. They raised the casket from the ground, with five men along each pole, and carried it down to the river. The rest of the villagers followed, chanting softly.

The Reverend held his Bible with both hands as he followed Moses and his entourage to the water's edge. The tribe's ancient Holy Man, using his traditional wooden talking stick like an extra leg, shadowed them, watching the Reverend very closely — and more than a little suspiciously. Despite his quiet, peaceful countenance, the Reverend was a tall and powerful man who looked as though he would be very dangerous if angered. Frankly, the Holy Man didn't trust him at all.

"I mourn the passing of your father, Moses, and pray for you in your time to lead," the Reverend said stentoriously.

Moses nodded politely, trying not to make it obvious that he also disliked, and distrusted, the man.

"Thank you for sharing your food," the Reverend said. "I will return the favor."

Moses waved that aside. "I expect nothing in return, Godman." He turned and ges-

18

tured toward Lily, who came forward with some intricate wooden carvings, which she tried to present to the Reverend as gifts.

The Reverend touched her head, declining the offer.

"To refuse is an insult," Lily said stiffly.

The Reverend put on a quick smile and took the gifts, nodding his thanks. Then, he turned the rather patronizing smile on Moses.

"There is something of yours that I want very badly," he said.

Moses tilted his head, curious.

"Your soul, Moses," the Reverend said solemnly. "Your soul."

Since that was an insult to the validity of his own religion and culture, Moses stiffened. "Safe trip back," he said, and turned to join his fellow villagers again.

Not one to give up, the Reverend was right behind him. "Do you ever wonder why God punishes you, Moses?"

"No," Moses said shortly. "We have done nothing to anger your God."

"But your people are facing starvation," the Reverend pointed out. "There must be a reason."

Moses stroked his large, bushy mustache, wanting to think about what he was going to say before he answered. "We've been here since the tide went out, Godman," he said finally. "We know these things. My grandfather spoke often of a time when the caribou would disappear. A time when the thunder in the earth will be followed by the coming of the White Wolf. If we are patient, we will be instructed how to restore the balance."

The Reverend made a face, unimpressed by this speech. "But that's only a story," he said. "You can't live your life like that.

Moses reached over and tapped the Reverend's Bible. "In your book, there are stories."

The Reverend had no comeback to that, so, frustrated, he decided to play his last card. "Moses," he said. "If you care for your people, take them to live with your relatives on the island."

Equally frustrated, Moses looked steadily at the Reverend. "You wear the same collar as the one before you, but your words are hollow," he said. "Reverend Michael understood our ways. He would never ask us to give up our land."

"Reverend Michael underestimated the

situation, Moses," the Reverend said, with a disinterested shrug. "Don't let the suffering continue. Your gods have failed you — but I won't. I can save you from this famine! Move your people before it's too late."

Moses continued looking at him, keeping his face completely expressionless so that he wouldn't betray any of his true emotions. "It is good you have a concern," he said in an even voice. "Thank you." He turned then, and walked back toward the Wolf House.

Giving up, the Reverend started to leave, but then felt Peter, the young warrior, staring at him, his eyes dark with anger.

"Hate will burn a hole in your heart, Peter," he said.

Peter didn't even blink. "I don't hate you, Godman. I pity you."

Infuriated by the tribe's rebelliousness, the Reverend walked away in disgust. He would be glad to get back to town, and be with people who thought the way he thought. These proud, stubborn Indians were just a waste of his valuable time.

The simple truth was that he really didn't care *what* happened to the Haida tribe.

That night, Moses slept fitfully in his compartment inside the Wolf House. As a smoky fire smoldered and the wind softly rattled the cedar-plank walls, he tossed and turned, fighting his way through a wild and complicated dream.

First, he heard the lonely howling of a wolf. He rose from his sleeping mat and saw White Fang standing in the doorway of the Wolf House, bright daylight behind him.

White Fang entered the Wolf House and padded over to Lily. She awoke from her sleep and left the Wolf House with White Fang, her steps as light and fluid as his were.

Mesmerized, Moses followed the pair out into the village. Up ahead, Lily ran into the woods. Then she stopped and stepped aside, revealing White Fang standing majestically in the middle of the path. He began to run and, in the dream, Lily and Moses followed, pursuing him like wolves.

They all ran through the woods, climbing over the rough ground, moving faster and faster. White Fang rounded a bend, and then stood at the edge of a cliff, looking back. He waited for Lily and Moses to join him, and then the three wolves-in-spirit looked over the edge. They saw a large herd of caribou milling about in the canyon below. There were enough caribou there to feed the starving Haida tribe for *years*.

Just then, Moses woke up from his dream. He sat bolt upright, staring blindly into the darkness.

The dream was a sign from the gods, and he would not ignore it.

Chapter 4

Moses shook his head a few times to clear it, unaware that Kat'rin was also awake and was looking at him curiously. Moses glanced around the dark room, his eyes barely pausing on the one non-Haida decoration — a faded American flag nailed to the wall.

The dream began to make more sense to him and he left his compartment, mumbling aloud to himself and dragging his blanket behind him. He tried not to wake any of the other sleepers as he approached where Lily slept.

Kat'rin followed him, her moccasins silent against the wooden floors as she stepped lightly over and around people.

Moses squatted down, sadly watching his niece sleep. Then, he reached forward and gave her a foot a gentle tug.

Lily opened her eyes, and when she saw the familiar silhouette, she knew who it was and smiled automatically, if sleepily.

"You came to me in my dream, Lily," Moses whispered. "You and the Wolf. You showed me the way."

Kat'rin joined Moses, kneeling by his side, her head bowed. The only sound in the room was the three of them breathing as Lily and Kat'rin waited for Moses to speak again.

"You will leave in the morning," he said.

Lily blinked, feeling as if she were dreaming herself. "Where am I going, Uncle?"

"To bring back the wolf," Moses said. "He will lead us to the caribou."

Her uncle was now the Haida Chief, and it was not proper to question him, but Lily couldn't help herself.

"Where will I look?" she asked.

"He will find *you*," Moses promised, and left, still dragging his blanket.

Uncertainly, Lily looked at Kat'rin for guidance.

"So tomorrow you will go," Kat'rin said, pleased that Lily had been chosen for this sacred duty. She put her arms out and enfolded Lily in a large hug.

If they could somehow find the long-lost caribou herd, the tribe would be saved.

Bright and early the next morning, Henry pulled his weathered raft into the water. He tied his heavy pack of gold sacks to the logs on one side and then loaded the rest of his gear.

White Fang, who was running back and forth skittishly, watched him from the shore.

Finished, Henry climbed onto the raft and whistled for him.

"Come on, boy," he said cheerfully. "Boat's sailing!"

White Fang hesitated, lifted one tentative paw and then backed away.

"What is it?" Henry asked. "It's safe. Look." He jumped up and down on the raft a few times to prove his point.

The raft listed slightly to one side and then bounced back up, floating beautifully.

"See?" Henry said.

White Fang stayed where he was, not convinced.

"You want to come, don't you?" Henry asked.

White Fang didn't move.

"Okay," Henry said. "Stay there, I'll come get you."

As he leaped onto the bank, White Fang reacted by instantly jumping onto the raft. Henry frowned, and did the same.

"Work with me, boy, will you?" he asked. Then he grabbed a long pole off the dock, pushing them out into the swift-moving current.

White Fang was still jittery, pacing around one corner of the raft.

"Relax," Henry said confidently. "This is the easy part."

White Fang just paced.

Down in the Haida village, Lily was inside her compartment, shivering in the morning chill. She held her shirt as Kat'rin carefully painted a red ritual sun on her bare chest to protect her on her journey.

"When the sun burst across the horizon," Kat'rin explained, "it swept away the dark.

That's when Ice Woman, your namesake, led her people away from the ice that crushed the villages. This is her crest. It will shield you from danger."

Lily nodded, taking strength from her adopted mother's words. "Thank you, Kat'rin."

Kat'rin smiled back at her and then stepped away, her painting completed. Lily waited until she was sure it was dry before lowering her shirt and smoothing the cloth down.

"Don't be fooled by what you see," Kat'rin warned her. "The wolf is a powerful being. He might not be visible to you. And he can change his shape. He may not be a wolf."

Lily thought about that, then frowned, suddenly perplexed. "What do I do when I *find* the White Wolf? What should I do with it?"

"You will know," Kat'rin said, sounding very wise, if enigmatic.

Lily nodded, doing her best to look determined even though she felt more confused than anything else.

Once she felt as prepared as she would

ever be, she went out to the stream where everyone else was waiting to see her off. Moses stood up front, with Kat'rin, Peter, and the Holy Man behind him, while the rest of the villagers encircled them. Most of the Indians were chanting, while others beat wooden drums or shook rattles. They wanted to give their "Ice Woman" a big send-off.

Lily stood by the water's edge, wearing a cedar bark hat, and feeling rather self-conscious.

Moses raised his arms and eyes to the sky. "Great Spirit, give her courage and strength to succeed — and guidance to bring her home," he prayed.

Nervously, Lily slipped as she tried to get into her canoe, Moses and Kat'rin both repressed the urge to help her. Lily took a deep breath, recovered, and stepped into the canoe. She felt for her wooden paddle and then pushed backwards into the current, letting it carry her down the stream.

The entire village watched, chanting and cheering, as she paddled away.

Moses glanced up at the sky, seeing a raven soar far above them. Since the

Haidas believed that the dead took animal forms in the afterlife, he was sure that the raven was a protective presence.

"Uncle, watch my niece," he said quietly "Keep her safe."

Lily's dangerous journey had begun.

Chapter 5

Henry and White Fang drifted down the river on the raft. Henry was enjoying the ride, but White Fang was still nervous, and Henry spoke to him soothingly, playing with the gold in one of the moose-hide sacks with one hand as he did. When he ran out of things to say, he sang some of the songs he knew instead, rolling a gold nugget between his fingers, feeling nothing but promise from the day ahead.

Even so, White Fang was agitated, as he prowled back and forth. His behavior was starting to make Henry a little uneasy. Henry looked around and suddenly realized that the water had risen and the current was stronger. Wanting to slow their speed, he quickly lowered the sail.

"It's moving right along," he said to White Fang. "Maybe we should walk for a bit."

Then, Henry lifted up his long wooden pole, and used it to push the raft towards the bank.

It would be better to be safe than sorry.

Lily was also trying to think positive thoughts as she paddled along in her canoe. She had no idea what she was supposed to see, but she was careful to keep searching the banks on either side, hoping to catch a glimpse of the mythical White Wolf.

Up ahead, she could see and hear rapids, so she guided her canoe to the bank and pulled it ashore. Then she looked around for the nearest tall tree and climbed it, wanting to be able to plan the safest possible route.

A flutter of wings startled her and she turned her head, seeing a raven perched on a nearby branch.

"You scared me, Uncle," she said chidingly. "What mischief are you up to today?"

The raven blinked.

"Have you seen our brother the Wolf?" Lily asked.

The raven stared.

"Well, when you do," Lily said, "tell him where I am."

With that, she climbed back down, took her gear out of the canoe, and started walking through the forest. It would be better to continue her journey on foot. The appearance of the raven must mean that she was heading in the right direction.

The raven swooped down from the tree, flew over her for a minute, and then veered over towards the river until he was out of sight.

Lily only hoped that he would be able to help her in her quest.

The river was getting much rougher, and Henry did his best to hide his fear from White Fang as he struggled to steer the raft over to the shore. He must not have done a very good job because White Fang was looking even more anxious than he had earlier.

A raven flew by, much lower than the birds usually flew. Instinctively, Henry followed its flight with his eyes, then returned his attention to the river as the raft bounced off the jagged rocks protruding from the water. The sharp edges of the rocks ripped at the ropes that held the craft together.

There was a roar like rolling thunder. When Henry looked downriver, his face fell. Raging rapids crashed through an S-shaped canyon — and the raft was heading straight for them.

"Oh, no!" Henry said, and he poled harder towards the bank.

But the raft was caught in the powerful current, and as Henry fought with the pole, it unexpectedly snapped, almost sending him into the churning waters. Henry was barely able to keep from being yanked overboard and he struggled to his feet, pulling White Fang against his body.

With his free arm, he held tight to the mast, watching helplessly as they floated towards the rapids. The raft was completely out of control.

"Hang on, boy," he said shakily. "We'll get through it."

The roar of the rapids had become deafening, and the raft spun helter-skelter. Henry hung onto White Fang as tightly as he could. He gasped as the water smashed over the sides of the raft, drenching both of them and sweeping all of his gear away. The pack of gold would be next, as the water battered at the rope securing it to the raft.

"Hang on!" Henry yelled.

Then, the raft was sucked into an outside current, and as they headed straight for the canyon wall, White Fang was jarred from his grasp. Henry lunged for him just as the raft slammed into the rocks. He missed, and it was too late to brace himself for the collision.

The raft crashed into a huge boulder and Henry was flipped overboard into the churning rapids. The wild current pulled him underneath the surface, and he disappeared from sight.

Henry was gone — and White Fang was now alone and helpless on the doomed raft.

Chapter 6

Coughing and choking on the freezing water, Henry struggled towards the surface, trying to find the raft. He managed to grab it with one hand, his fingers desperately raking at the pack of gold as he tried to pull himself aboard. But his head struck rock and he went limp. His body slid underneath the roiling water.

The raft, and the packs of gold — and White Fang — floated on without him. White Fang ran back and forth on the slippery logs, barking loudly as he looked for Henry in the churning froth.

From the forest, Lily heard the sound

and quickly moved towards the shore, all the while staring at the rapids ahead. She blinked her eyes in disbelief as she saw a wolf — White Fang — leap into the water from a raft, and float down the river, his paws flailing as he tried to swim.

It didn't seem possible, but she had found the White Wolf.

She looked around wildly, trying to think of a way to save him.

Floating just beyond the rapids was an ingenious Indian fishing contraption called a fish wheel. Made of willow branches, the skeleton of the twenty-five-foot-wide wheel spun in the current, only one third of it visible above the surface. There were netting compartments spread along the circumference. As the wheel turned, the nets scooped up fish and deposited them in a chute that ran into a holding pen.

Lily ran along the bank, watching White Fang. She screamed as he was yanked under the water by the current and pulled out of sight. She had found the White Wolf, only to lose him.

She was racing back and forth, frantically searching, when Henry, riding the fish wheel, rose miraculously out of the water like an apparition. His free arm seemed to wave her on as it flopped lifelessly across his chest.

Lily screamed again as he spun off the wheel and dropped face down in the chute. Mystified, she stared, a shocked witness to the Wolf's power. Kat'rin was right — he *was* a shape-changer! The Wolf went into the water and came back a man. Not only had he become a man, but he had changed into a *white man*.

Cautiously, she approached the fish wheel, where Henry's unconscious body was still floating.

In the meantime, White Fang's head had popped to the surface out in the middle of the river. He paddled hard, struggling to breathe as the rapids carried him farther and farther downstream. He was in danger of drowning, and there was no one to save him.

Back by the fish wheel, Lily moved tentatively to Henry's side. He was sprawled facedown in the mud, and she gazed at him with a mixture of fascination and repulsion.

A *white* man?" she said, unbelievingly.

The shape-changer had not taken a form her fellow tribe members would have expected.

*   *   *

White Fang floated for miles until finally his battered body was washed up onto the rocks by the edge of the river. At first, he looked as though he might be dead, but then he opened his eyes blearily.

He lay there for a minute, then jerked up and limped weakly upstream, scared and confused. Where was Henry? He searched for the boy's scent, his nose in the air. He couldn't find it and, exhausted, he sank down on his haunches in the mud to rest.

Then, mourning his loss, he rocked back and howled, over and over and over.

Battered and bruised, Henry woke up in a fog of pain to find Lily kneeling beside him, rocking in a trance as she sang a haunting Haida healing song. She was the most beautiful thing he had ever seen, and he wondered if she could be a heavenly vision.

Just before he passed out again, he saw pieces of his raft smashed against the bank, and he remembered what had happened.

"White Fang!" he called, and then fainted.

He had lost his dearest friend.

Chapter 7

After resting alone for a while, White Fang staggered up and wandered around, looking for shelter. He found a cave that smelled as if it had once been a wolf den. He collapsed inside on the dirt floor and fell asleep.

He had been sleeping for quite a while when he was awakened by some squeaky growls. Backing away from him were two curious ten-week-old wolf cubs. He was too tired to approach them, so he stayed where he was.

One of the cubs got brave and came closer to sniff at him. White Fang licked him in greeting and the cub jerked back, his hackles raised. He looked at the other cub and they both ran out of the cave, spooked.

Limping badly, White Fang followed them out into the woods. He kept his distance as he watched the wolf cubs run straight to their seven-member pack. The wolves were all sharing a recent kill and White Fang saw the black wolf who was the leader, his mate who was the cubs' mother, two other adult males, and a two-year-old cinnamon-colored female.

The cinnamon female was the only wolf to look up. When she spotted White Fang, she tilted her head. Injured and weak, White Fang retreated, limping back into the protection of the woods. In his condition, he would never be able to handle any sort of confrontation with the male wolves.

Knowing that he needed something to eat if he was going to get his strength back, he began to forage for food. First, he chased a rabbit, using the fastest limp he could manage, but the rabbit outdistanced him easily. Then he found a ferret, which beat him to a hole in a tree and escaped with very little difficulty.

Today, White Fang would go hungry.

What he didn't know was that the cinnamon wolf had been watching his struggle the entire time. After he had limped back to the old wolf den to rest, she caught a duck and brought it to the opening of the cave. She dropped it on the ground, and quickly scampered away.

Hearing a noise, White Fang came out and saw her running off. He also saw the dinner she had left him. He watched her until her form had disappeared into the forest. Then he picked up the duck and carried it back inside the den.

He wouldn't go hungry, after all.

Henry slept fitfully through the night, his body stirring as though he were caught in a nightmare. Whenever he awoke, for a few sleep-blurred moments, he would catch a glimpse of Lily, sitting by a crackling fire, singing the Haida healing song. Then he would drop off again into his restless sleep.

The next time he woke up, the sun was bright in his eyes and he could feel his body moving. He moaned and squinted in the sunshine, trying to figure out where he was, and why he felt as though he were floating.

"What?" he asked vaguely. "What — what happened?" He propped himself up on his elbows and saw that he was lying in a canoe — and that the beautiful girl was paddling it.

Lily stiffened, not having planned on conversation with the shape-changer yet.

"You speak English?" he asked.

She hesitated, holding her paddle just above the rippling water.

"Who are you?" Henry asked.

"Lily," she said, after a pause.

He repeated the name softly. "Lily." Then he tried to sit up enough to see exactly where on the river they were. "You pulled me out? Where are we going?"

"To my village," she answered.

Henry frowned, a little perplexed by this. "We anywhere near Dawson?"

Lily shook her head. "You must rest now," she said.

He nodded, still weak, and lay back in the canoe, allowing his mind to float along with it. Watching the trees gliding by overhead, being transported by a beautiful Indian girl — it was almost like being in a dream.

Then he remembered what had happened and sat upright.

"Did you see a wolf?" he asked urgently.

Lily nodded.

"Did he go in the water?" Henry asked.

Lily nodded again.

Henry swallowed. "Did he come back up?"

Lily nodded.

Henry let out a relieved breath, glad that his worst fears hadn't been confirmed. "Where is he?"

Lily smiled and pointed at him.

"*Me?*" Henry said.

Lily nodded.

He shook his head, confused by this. "I don't understand."

"You will," Lily said enigmatically.

That didn't make any sense to him, but Henry decided to ignore it. "Did he get out?" he asked. "The wolf?"

Lily shook her head.

"No!" Henry whispered, his eyes widening in disbelief and his voice choking with emotion. "White Fang . . ." He slumped back down in the canoe, grieving for his lost friend.

He lay there for a long time, then looked up dully from his reverie, and watched Lily as she sat in the back of the canoe, her paddle sure and silent. Somehow, it was a soothing sight. He noticed three parallel scars on her inner forearm, which were both fascinating and foreboding. He was going to ask what they were when he remembered something else.

"My gold!" he said, sitting up so swiftly that he almost tipped the canoe over. "I lost my gold!"

"Sit down!" Lily ordered, struggling to keep the canoe from capsizing.

"We gotta go back," Henry said weakly.

Lily frowned at him, shaking her head. "Be still."

Henry covered his face miserably with his hands. "It's somewhere in this river."

"The village is close now," Lily said, trying to soothe him.

"You don't understand," Henry said, his voice bereft. "That was next year's supplies. I've got nothing. Everything I worked for — it's gone." And, of course, his best friend was gone, too. "*Everything*," he said, his voice heavy with despair.

He sat there, shaking his head, and mumbling unhappily to himself.

Seeing his self-pity and his love for his

lost gold only confirmed Lily's worst prejudices about the white man.

Despite what she had seen, could this *really* be the White Wolf?

More importantly, if he *wasn't* the White Wolf, who exactly *was* she bringing to her village?

Chapter 8

When he woke up that same morning, White Fang felt much better and found that his limp had improved. Until he came up with a better strategy, he decided to trail after the wolf pack.

He ran along the top of a ridge, looking at the pack below. They were running and playing, and Cinnamon was frolicking more than any of the others. The pack never stopped moving and White Fang kept out of sight as he followed them.

Catching an animal scent that might lead him to a meal, he put his nose to the ground, and trailed the odor. This distracted him enough that when the black wolf unexpectedly leaped out of the woods into his path, White Fang stood stock-still for a minute.

Then, in a battle of flying fur and gnashing teeth, White Fang made the first move, attacking the black wolf and returning instinctively to the fighting ways that had long lain dormant in him. He didn't like to fight — but he still knew how.

When the other two male wolves appeared ready to join the fray, White Fang didn't stand a chance, and knew he had to make a hasty retreat. He ran at least a hundred yards away and then turned back to watch the pack, united once more, run off.

But before they left, Cinnamon looked back at him with compassion. Still she turned and followed her family.

White Fang, not dismayed, followed them, too — although from a safe distance. He was not going to let her go that easily.

When the pack crossed the river by running along a felled tree, White Fang was right behind them. Reaching the far side, he realized he was near the place where the raft had capsized, and he headed upstream in search of Henry.

Cinnamon saw him going, and knew that it was time for her to choose between the lone wolf and the pack. She hesitated, and then made her choice, White Fang.

The black wolf saw this, and led the pack in the same direction. He would not give up Cinnamon easily, either.

In the meantime, White Fang had come across the fish wheel that had saved Henry's life, and the remains of the camp where Lily had watched and chanted over him through the long night. He picked up Henry's scent and circled the camp once with his nose to the ground before following the trail into the forest.

Down in the Haida village, it was almost sunset and Moses was asleep just outside the Wolf House. He was sitting on a bench with his back against the wall, wrapped in an old blanket. An ancient dog was curled up asleep at his feet.

The villagers moved past them with quiet reverence, careful not to awaken their chief.

Suddenly, Moses jerked upright and looked around as if he had heard something. The dog also jumped up and started barking. Moses moved quickly to the entrance of the Wolf House and stuck his head inside.

"To the water!" he shouted. "She is here! The canoe is arriving!"

He ran towards the water's edge and waded in above his knees, peering anxiously upstream. Behind him, the villagers were gathering. In preparation for a celebration ceremony, the Holy Man held ropes tied to the waists of five young men, including Peter, who were now dressed as Wolf Boys, complete with wolf masks.

Moses saw a canoe approaching, turned proudly, and started chanting to the villagers. They all joined in, picking up his rhythm. Drums pounded and whistles pierced the air, creating a tremendous din. The Holy Man snapped the ropes and the Wolf Boys danced by the just-lit bonfire.

From the canoe, Henry caught sight of the village and the loud reception party awaiting them.

"What's that all about?" he asked uneasily.

"You," Lily said.

He swallowed apprehensively as Lily

slowed the canoe down and stood up, raising her arms to the sky.

Moses quieted the villagers and cupped his hand around his mouth, shouting to her in ceremonial greeting. "Who are you! Why have you come!"

"I am Ice Woman of the river people!" Lily responded. "I bring with me the White Wolf!"

"Come ashore!" Moses said in a commanding voice.

Lily sat down and paddled them to shore while Henry watched, stunned by her power and mysterious allure.

Moses waded up to meet the canoe and studied Henry warily. He certainly had not expected Lily to return with a white man.

Sensing this, Henry gave him a broad, if nervous, smile.

When the villagers saw that a white boy was their savior, their excitement diminished and the Wolf Boys stopped dancing. Peter was the first to remove his mask and stare at Henry, perplexed.

Moses turned to Lily in consternation. "Who is this, Lily?"

"This is the one, Uncle," Lily said.

"This *boy?*" Moses asked.

Lily nodded. "I saw the change. The wolf went under the water." She gestured towards Henry. "The boy came back up."

Henry frowned, suspecting that a pretty serious mistake was being made here. "Now, wait just a minute," he said. "No one changed into anything. The wolf was my friend, and . . ." his voice grew sad — "I lost him in the river. He lived with me."

"You live with the wolf?" Moses asked suspiciously.

"Yes, sir," Henry said.

Now Moses allowed himself a small smile. "This is very good." He knew that there was truth somewhere in all of this, and was open to pursuing it. "Welcome to our village. I am Moses Joseph. Chief of the Haidas."

"Henry Casey," Henry said. "San Francisco."

"Henry Casey," Moses repeated. "Funny name."

"Well — thank you" Henry said, uncertainly.

Moses pulled the canoe the rest of the way to shore and Henry and Lily climbed out. Moses chanted to keep their spirits up as he led them through the gauntlet of villagers to the Wolf House.

Henry allowed himself to be led, but he couldn't help feeling uncomfortable. He had a feeling that he was in *way* over his head.

Chapter 9

That night a ceremony was held around the fire pit in the Wolf House, and all the villagers gathered inside to watch. Water shaken from cedar boughs was sprinkled over the hot coals in an abalone shell. As the smoke rose, Moses washed his hands in it, doing a purification ritual.

Scared, fascinated, and confused, Henry stared at the Chief's magic hands as they wafted the smoke with an eagle feather, directing it towards his face until the clouds circled his head. Then Moses sat back and looked at Lily.

She repeated the ritual and returned to her place. Moses now nodded at Henry, who hesitated, not sure what he was supposed to do. Lily caught his eye and signaled for him to move forward. Henry did so, knelt down, imitated their movements, and sat back in his place with a nervous cough.

The villagers witnessed all of this, their expressions deadly serious. Kat'rin and Peter were sitting up in the front. While Kat'rin looked happy, Peter's face and body language were blatantly skeptical.

"At the time of my grandfather's grandfather," Moses began, "our mother the earth shook, and part of the Mountain you call Devil's Thumb broke off and landed on their village. Many of our people died. But, in return, the creator gave us the caribou. Every year, they come to us from Devil's Thumb. For this reason, we respect the Mountain and do not go there."

The villagers nodded, listening intently even though it was a story they already knew. This tale was only new to Henry.

Moses took a deep breath before going on. "For two years now, the caribou have not returned. Eight hunters went to find them and they, too, have vanished. Without the caribou, the balance in our lives is gone. My people starve, die . . . move away."

Henry looked around at the haggard faces of the villagers, realizing that they *were* starving.

"If my dream showed me the way of this Godman, I'd ask my people to move," Moses went on. "But the dream told of the White Wolf who would lead us to the caribou. . . ." He cocked his chin jauntily in Henry's direction. "And now, Henry Casey — you are here."

"*Me?*" Henry swallowed hard, mortified. "You've got the wrong man, sir. I'm not much of a hunter. I'm more of a — a miner."

The elders were shocked by his disrespect. Some of the women chuckled derisively. Lily glared at them, and they subsided.

"That's very interesting," Moses said with a smile.

"*Really*," Henry insisted. "That wolf your niece saw was a pet. Now *he* was a hunter. He was something. But he's gone now."

Moses shrugged. "He could be alive inside you. The wolf has the power to change."

"Into *me?*" Henry asked.

Moses nodded.

"Why would he do that?" Henry asked, doubtfully. He wanted more than anything for White Fang to be alive, but he *knew* that the wolf wasn't inside of him.

"He's clever," Moses said. "He'd let us know."

Henry didn't answer right away, not wanting to hurt the old chief's feelings. "I guess it's okay to believe that, sir, but I don't," he said finally. "I'm no wolf, sir. I'm a man. That's all."

A number of the villagers tittered and Lily, embarrassed and angered, pushed between them and stalked out of the Wolf House.

Henry got up to follow her. "Lily, wait!"

Peter, his arms folded, stepped in front of Henry, blocking his way.

Seeing potential conflict, Moses rose to his feet.

"The boy is free to leave when he wishes," he said.

"Thank you," Henry said. "I need supplies, and — I have to wire San Francisco for money. There must be a town near here?"

Moses nodded. "When you are ready, we can show you the way."

"Well, it's too late now," Henry said, since it was long after sundown. "If it's okay with you, I'll, uh, stay here tonight and leave in the morning?"

"Good idea," Moses answered. "Kat'rin can show you where to lie down. Sleep now, Henry Casey. We can talk again tomorrow."

As the Chief moved towards his sleeping area, the villagers dispersed in virtual silence, staring at Henry as they did. The stares were not exactly friendly.

Henry, feeling self-conscious, squatted down by the fire to warm his hands. "Nice old guy, huh?" he said, indicating the direction that Moses had gone.

Peter took offense at this, and scowled at him. "Old guy is my *father*," he said. "Who are *you* in his house?"

Henry got up, feeling both confused and threatened, but ready to defend himself.

Just in time, Kat'rin appeared, grabbed him by the arm and led him away.

"I didn't mean anything," Henry said defensively.

Kat'rin just shook her head and ushered him out.

Although she showed him to a nice sleeping area and did her best to make him feel welcome, Henry stayed awake long after everyone else had fallen asleep. Despondent, he leaned against the wall, wrapped in a blanket and staring into the shadows. All around him he saw paintings and carvings of wolves. Naturally, they reminded him of White Fang and he got even sadder.

"White Fang," he said softly, feeling very much like crying. Then he realized that he wasn't alone and looked up to see Lily standing over him, her eyes filled with disdain.

"I should have known," she said, practically spitting the words out. "You're a white man — you don't see. . . ." She dropped a small coin at his feet. "This *coin* has as much life as you do."

He looked at her, stunned by the rebuke. "Hey, I didn't *ask* you to bring me here."

"I sang the healing song for you," she said accusingly.

Henry frowned. "What's that supposed to mean?"

"I gave you back your life," she said. "Now your life belongs to me."

Henry started to get up. "Wait a minute — "

"But there *is* no life in a coin," she said. "So, go! I throw you away."

He looked down at the coin and then back at her, shaking his head. "You believe that stuff?"

"All *you* believe in is your gold," she said.

Henry shook his head again, losing patience with this entire situation. "Look, whatever you did, I'm grateful, but I'm not going to some godforsaken place to hunt caribou, okay?"

"We thought you were the White Wolf," Lily said bitterly.

Henry shrugged. "Sorry."

Lily nodded, scornfully. "The wolf is a great hunter with a warrior's heart. *You* are like every other white man."

He might not be the wolf, but that didn't make him the tribe's enemy, either. "Lily," he said. "You're wrong."

She looked at him challengingly. "Then

find the caribou, Henry Casey." She turned and walked away, without another word.

Henry couldn't help thinking that he might have been better off if she'd just *left* him in the stupid river to drown.

Chapter 10

When Henry walked out of the Wolf House the next morning, he saw Lily squatting down by the water's edge. He went over to her and was followed by a curious group of women and children. She was watching Moses take his morning constitutional. He was sitting up to his neck in the water, singing quietly to himself.

The look she gave Henry was distinctly chilly, but he crouched down next to her, anyway.

"My father takes cold showers every morning," he volunteered. "He sings, too. Drives my mother crazy." He frowned, worried that the meaning of that phrase might get lost in the translation. "Well, not really *crazy*." He laughed, but stopped quickly.

Lily shook her head, irritated, and there was an awkward pause.

"I came to say good-bye," Henry said.

"Good-bye," Lily said, her voice flat.

Henry sighed, running one hand back through his unruly hair. "I wanted to straighten something out."

Lily looked at him guardedly.

"I don't know what kind of white people you've run into," Henry said, "but we're not all the same."

She didn't respond.

He took a deep breath, and tried again. "There may be some bad men coming through up here, but I'm not one of them."

Lily just stared straight ahead.

"Maybe *you're* the one who doesn't see," he said.

She turned away from him completely.

"Lily . . ." He reached out and touched her arm. "You expect me to believe everything you believe. I can't do that."

Peter came striding over from the Wolf House and stood purposefully between them.

"I was talking to Lily," Henry said stiffly. "Right, Lily?"

She faced away from both of them.

"Get out of the way," Henry said to Peter.

"Why are you still here?" Peter asked pugnaciously.

Frustrated, Henry stood up and tried to move around him to get to Lily. Peter was taller and easily blocked his way. Like little boys in a playground, they moved and countermoved until Henry got tired of the charade and gave Peter a hard shove.

Peter quickly slapped one hand behind Henry's neck and grabbed his wrist with the other, trying to force Henry to his knees in the traditional Haida strength game. Henry grabbed Peter's shoulders, struggling to keep his balance as they tried to outmuscle each other.

"Stop, Peter!" Lily yelled. "You shame your father."

Moses heard the commotion and rushed out of the water, dripping wet. "Peter! Peter!"

Hearing his voice, Peter instantly let Henry go and offered him his hand. Henry hesitated, but then took it and stood up.

Peter promptly dropped his hand and walked swiftly away.

"He was testing you," Moses said. "He meant you no harm."

Lily handed the Chief a green willow branch and he whipped himself across the back to help his circulation.

"Peter has reasons to be angry," Moses continued. "His brother Matthew did not return from the hunt." Still whipping himself with the branch, he walked off with Lily, then stopped to look back at Henry. "Come. The Holy Man is waiting."

Henry wasn't sure what that meant, but ran to catch up with them. He walked with them to a small domed shack, which was built into the side of a hill with a low tunnel for an entrance. Moses knelt briefly, then looked at Henry.

"Take off your clothes," he said, after dropping the blanket that was around his waist.

Henry shook his head vehemently. "That's okay. I'll keep 'em on."

Moses looked baffled by that, but crawled through the entrance. Henry smiled uneasily at Lily, knelt down, and went after him.

They had only been inside for a few seconds when Henry knew why Moses had told him to take off his clothes. He was in a ceremonial sweathouse. Since he was fully dressed, he suffered greatly in the heat, in stark contrast with the nakedness of Moses and the Holy Man, who was known to the tribe as Sshaga.

As an assistant pounded a drum, Sshaga shook a rattle, and felt Henry's head with his brittle old fingers, his eyes closed to help him "see." The ancient Holy Man spoke only Haida, and Moses translated for Henry.

"You will hear the moans of the ones who crossed over before their time," Moses said. "You will feel the silent sting of death brush near you, be turned around, yet find your way to the highest point. There you will see both sides of the world and not be alone. When you enter the heart of the mountain, you will face two enemies: yourself and one whose face remains in shadows. Then you will become one with the Wolf."

Finished, Sshaga let go of Henry's head and took the boy's hands in his as he sat back and opened his eyes. Henry, forgetting how overheated he was, stared into Sshaga's luminous eyes, transfixed — and saw the eyes of the Wolf staring back at him. Then, the Holy Man spoke some more Haida and Moses translated.

"Step inside me," Moses said. "Walk in my dream. See what I see."

Scared, and feeling as though he had been set up, Henry jerked his hands away.

"Why are you doing this?" he asked, unable to keep his voice from shaking slightly.

Moses shrugged. "Your truth is there."

"My truth?" Henry said disbelievingly. "These are modern times, sir — you can't run your life like this."

"It is the way we live," Moses said simply.

Henry shook his head. "Well, *I* don't."

Moses saw through his anger to his fear, and reached out towards him.

"Sorry," Henry said. "I've got my own problems, sir." He turned around and crawled outside, shaken by Sshaga's prophesy. He was going to run away, but realized that he didn't know where he was, and stopped in confusion.

"Go, Henry Casey," Moses said calmly. "Do what you have to do. The wolf will find you." He motioned for Lily with one hand. "And when you think of us, Henry, think with your heart."

Henry nodded, although the only thing he was really thinking about was getting *away* from this place — forever.

Obeying Moses' orders, Lily led Henry through the woods to show him the way to town.

"Listen, Lily," he explained. "Where I come from, gold makes you somebody special." Henry sounded as if he might be trying to convince *himself* too. "It makes your dreams come true. If you've got enough gold, you can go anywhere, do anything — you can have everything you ever wanted. *And I had that much gold* — before I lost it. I would've been a rich man."

Lily said nothing at all, not wanting to betray what she was feeling. She just led Henry to a faint path by the river and pointed upstream.

"Stay with the path," she said. "Before dark, you will come to it."

"Thanks," Henry was going to start off, but then hung back for a minute. "I won't forget what you did for me. I wish I could help you."

"Empty words," she said without much interest.

"No," Henry insisted. "They're not."

"You would do anything for your gold," Lily said, "but nothing for my people."

Henry shook his head.

"You think of only yourself," Lily said.

"Yeah," Henry agreed. "Because if I don't, no one else will." The words sounded harsh and he stopped, a little ashamed of himself. "Maybe you're right. Maybe I'm not a hunter or a warrior — and maybe I don't belong here. Maybe — " He looked at her, losing his train of thought at the sight of her deep, dark, unforgiving eyes. It was much too easy for him to get lost in those eyes.

The gulf between them seemed enormous, and he sighed painfully.

"Why do you have to be so pretty," he said.

Lily didn't bend for a second. "I was made that way. Now go. Don't come back."

With that, she turned and ran back to the Haida village, disappearing over the rise.

He listened to her footsteps fade until all he could hear in the empty silence was the wind. The sound only heightened his loneliness, but he forced himself down the path. It was time to go back where he belonged.

His only problem was that he was no longer sure exactly where that *was*.

Chapter 11

White Fang had followed Henry's scent all through the night until he finally tracked it to the Haida village. He stopped, seeing the smoke from the various cooking and heating fires, as well as the tops of totem poles. He looked back and saw Cinnamon still behind him, but keeping her distance.

The pack caught up to her then and they all changed direction, staying well clear of the village.

White Fang, on the other hand, headed straight towards it.

After all, Henry was there.

* * *

As Henry walked along the lonely path, he felt the earth shaking under his feet and heard the pounding of horses' hooves ahead of him.

He saw three ragged American soldiers on horseback waiting alongside a hilltop. Another man who seemed to be wearing the garb of a preacher rode towards them, and the men talked. They were too far away for Henry to be able to hear what they were saying, but somehow, the meeting looked ominous.

Then he watched as the four men spurred their steeds and galloped off. It was obvious that the men were after *something*.

Henry kept walking and finally reached the mining town. It was his first sight of civilization in a long time, but the place looked like a ghost town. The boarding house was practically falling down and the stable and combination general store-barber shop-eatery didn't look much better. There was also a Protestant church, its wall and roof storm-battered and neglected.

Henry moved cautiously down the dusty street, seeing angry and disillusioned faces everywhere. These were men who had come to Alaska to make their fortunes and had had their dreams crushed. It was the dark side of gold fever.

A man wheeled down the street on a bike, delivering the mail. At the sight of him the miners' eyes brightened. Starved for news, they rose and followed the man as if he were the Pied Piper.

"What's the word, Adam John?" one asked.

"Gold in Nome!" Adam John said. "Three Swedes took out six hundred dollars in ten hours!"

He parked his bike by the general store and took off his goggles. He was in his mid-fifties and very striking, with long gray-streaked black hair framing his face. He was half Irish and half Haida — and an odd-looking combination of the two.

Henry watched him, fascinated.

"Read for yourself," Adam John said, and flipped a newspaper to the nearest miner.

But the miners had lost interest in mail. Looks of mistrust passed between the gold-hungry strangers. The news of gold in Nome had brought their gold rush fever back, and they moved off in separate directions to grab their belongings and take off.

The general store's proprietor, Heath, came outside as Adam John sorted through the mail. Heath was Norwegian and in his forties, with very bad teeth.

"Where dem bottom-feeders goin'?" he asked, indicating the miners.

"Nome," Adam John answered.

Within seconds, the few miners left in town were packed up and leaving the sinking ship. Henry was tempted to go with them, his own appetite for gold still strong.

Heath shook his head and spit into the dirt. "Time they get there, most be dead, and there won't be room for what's left to make camp."

Adam John saw that Henry was struggling with what to do. "You ain't going?"

The emerging man in the boy put the dream to rest, and Henry shook his head. "Just got here," he said.

Heath looked him over critically, and spit again.

"Who are you, boy?" Adam John asked.

"Name's Henry Casey," Henry said.

"Got a claim, north of here. I was on my way to Dawson to make a deposit, but I wrecked my raft on the river. I lost everything." He shook his head unhappily, thinking about White Fang. *"Everything."*

"Then you're lucky," Adam John said.

Henry stared at him in some confusion.

"You're still alive," Adam John said, and went back to sorting his mail.

Back in the Haida village, Moses, Kat'rin, and Lily sat quietly by the edge of the water with the others, watching the sunset.

Lily glanced down the shoreline, and couldn't believe her eyes.

"That's him, Uncle," she said wonderingly. "That's the Wolf."

Moses turned and saw White Fang, not even twenty yards away. He studied the wolf, fitting together another piece to the puzzle of his dream.

"The other half," he said. "Good sign."

He stood up and went towards the wolf. At first, White Fang growled, but something about Moses' countenance calmed him and he allowed the old chief to touch him.

Moses smiled. "Don't be afraid, my brother."

Peter was just coming out of the Wolf House and he gasped when he saw his father standing so close to a wolf. He looked around for some sort of weapon and White Fang instantly reacted to the threat, darting away into the night.

Moses just smiled. He knew that the White Wolf would be back.

Henry followed Adam John and Heath into the general store, and sat down to the biggest meal Heath could rustle up. He explained what had happened to him while the two older men listened with great interest.

"Anyway," Henry said, wrapping up the story. "I figured the best thing I could do for them was keep moving. At least I wouldn't be eating their food. Then, Lily —"

Heath interrupted. "Lily?"

"The Indian girl," Henry said, unable to disguise the longing in his voice.

Heath laughed. "Dat's the only kind they got out there."

Henry shrugged, embarrassed. "Well,

she walked me to the stream and pointed me here. And — here I am."

Adam John and Heath paused to digest the story.

"Why didn't you stay and help them?" Adam John asked.

"Why? I'll tell you why." Henry paused. "You're Indian, right?"

Adam John nodded patiently.

"I thought so," Henry said, also nodding. "So you probably understand them a lot better than I do. They're into some strange stuff out there — believing their dreams like they do. They need help." Then, he remembered something. "I saw soldiers coming in. Where are they quartered?"

Adam John and Heath looked at each other.

"Army's way out in Dawson," Heath said.

Henry shook his head. "No. I *just* saw them, they — "

"Must've been passin' through," Heath said, cutting him off. "There's no law out here."

It still didn't seem right, and Henry frowned.

"So now you'll go home and forget these

people who helped you," Adam John said quietly.

Henry shrugged, feeling defensive again. "If I thought I could help them, I would."

"*They* think you can," Adam John pointed out.

"*They* think I'm the White Wolf," Henry reminded him.

Adam John looked at him for a long silent minute. "Maybe you are," he said.

Chapter 12

Unnerved by the seriousness in Adam John's eyes, Henry couldn't quite look at him. So Adam John just gave him a nod and left the store.

"Don't mind him, kid," Heath said, going through the packages lying beside the mail bag. "Old Adam John's harmless, just a mite sensitive. His mama come from that village."

Henry looked at him curiously. "Really?"

Heath nodded. "There used to be close to five hundred Haidas out here. Now there ain't but fifty or so left, and half of them lives up behind the church."

"What happened to the others?" Henry asked.

Heath shrugged. "Smallpox. White man's gift to the Indian."

Henry thought about that — and about Lily. She really had every right to be bitter.

Later, when darkness had fallen, he left the store and went outside. There was a fire going behind the church and he headed towards it. Crossing the street, he noticed his old enemy from the cabin, Halverson, lying asleep in the alley in a drunken stupor. Without White Fang by his side, he made a point of steering clear.

He easily found the Indian settlement behind the church and saw about twenty Haidas — almost half of Moses' people — either huddling by the fire or staring watchfully from small cramped Army tents. It was clear that they were living from handout to handout — when they were lucky.

The back door of the church opened and the Reverend looked out with a foreboding glare in his eyes. He saw Henry, and relaxed slightly.

"Sad, isn't it?" he said.

Henry didn't know how to answer, so he just shrugged.

The Reverend frowned and closed the door.

Depressed by the downtrodden settlement, Henry wandered around the mining camp, wrestling with his conscience. He heard a flute playing inside the stable and tentatively went inside.

There were eight stalls — and only two mules boarding in there. The rear door was ajar and Henry could see the dancing light of a fire outside. He headed towards it and saw Adam John sitting by the fire, satyr-like, playing a flute.

Henry sat down to listen and noticed the wolf skin on which Adam John was sitting. He reached out, touching it sadly.

"You're lucky to be friends with a wolf," Adam John said. "Not many are."

Henry pulled his hand back and put it in his pocket.

They sat in silence, and Adam John took out a knife, whittling away at his flute.

"I didn't mean to be disrespectful," Henry said. "I didn't know they were your people."

Without answering, Adam John poured

him a steaming cup of coffee, and watched him sip the hot liquid.

"Do you believe in God, Henry Casey?" he asked.

Henry shrugged. "Much as the next man, I guess."

"We Haidas believe the Raven is the Creator," Adam John said, staring at the fire. "And we believe the spirit of an animal can enter a man. Strange things, maybe."

Henry nodded hesitantly.

"But not strange for us," Adam John said.

Henry got the message, and lowered his eyes.

"Trust what's inside, boy," Adam John said quietly, and touched his chest. "Don't fear what you can't understand."

Henry was still afraid, but he found himself nodding.

That night, he slept in the stable. At one point, something spooked the mule in the next stall, and it started braying and bucking. Henry woke up, his heart racing, but there was nothing there. Finally, he went back to sleep.

He began to dream, and the dream started with the chilling howl of a wolf. In the dream, he sat bolt upright and saw White Fang standing in the doorway. Henry followed him out of the barn and into bright sunlight.

Ahead of him was the same path that Moses had dreamed about. White Fang was running into the woods and Henry ran after him, finding himself moving low to the ground, like a wolf. He ran faster than he ever had, with grace and agility he had never felt before.

He ran to the edge of the same cliff Moses had seen, where White Fang was waiting. He pushed past the wolf, looked down — and saw the caribou, *exactly as Moses had told him*.

Henry woke up, shouting "White Fang!," and was stunned to find himself on all fours, at the edge of a road outside town. He looked around in a panic, and then down at his wet feet. He had no idea how he had gotten there — or even where he was — but he knew that he was more afraid than he had ever been.

It was barely dawn, and he ran back to the mining town, racing into the stable. He tore through the building as though he were being chased by the Devil and charged at Adam John, grabbing him by the jacket and yanking him to his feet.

"What did you do to me?" he demanded.

"I-I did nothing, boy," Adam John said, stuttering slightly.

Henry stared at him, breathing hard. "I'm losing my mind, aren't I?"

"No," Adam John said. "Stop fighting it. You've been touched, boy."

"But I don't want to be!" Henry yelled and ran back through the stable to the main street.

He stormed down the road, completely bewildered, and then stopped dead in his tracks as though something from above had grabbed him by the shoulders.

His internal battle was reaching a crescendo. He hyperventilated, looking up and down the empty street, trying to figure out where he could go to get away from all of this.

Afraid that he was losing his grip on reality, he looked around, searching for something — *anything* — to hold onto. He spotted the cross at the top of the church and walked toward it. He sat down on the muddy walkway below the church stairs.

He buried his head in his hands, overcome with self-pity and defeat.

Then, feeling someone's eyes on him, he lifted his head. There, standing a few yards away, was a ragged little Haida boy. The boy was maybe five years old and he stared at Henry with wide eyes full of innocence and hurt. He did not avert his gaze, but simply stood there in silent witness to Henry's turmoil.

Henry looked back at him and, for a moment, everything was still.

Then, a mother called the boy. Henry looked at her, and realized that he had seen this boy and mother before in his dreams — but they were now homeless. They desperately needed his help. *All* of the Haidas did.

And then, very clearly, Henry knew what it was that he must do.

He walked back to the stable, his stride determined and purposeful. Adam John was working on his bike, and he looked up when he heard Henry come in.

"I'm going back," Henry said.

Chapter 13

Adam John was very pleased by Henry's decision, and accompanied him to the general store so he could make some final arrangements. Henry was working on a telegram to send to San Francisco when the Reverend walked in and exchanged pleasantries with Heath and Adam John.

Henry read his telegram one last time and handed it to Heath to send. He didn't want to ask his family for money, but he didn't have much choice.

"Was there any mail for me yesterday?" the Reverend asked.

Adam John shook his head. "One for Reverend Michael."

"I'll take that," the Reverend said quickly.

Adam John frowned, but gave it to him.

"How long you figure?" Henry asked, indicating the telegram.

"Be there in two days, maybe three," Heath guessed. "When your money gets back . . . that's another story."

"At least a week," Adam John said. "Maybe more."

Henry bit his lip, thinking. "Could I get some credit? I'm leaving for the village tomorrow, and I was hoping I could take some food out there."

Heath looked over at the now-attentive Reverend before returning his attention to Henry. "Sorry, boy. No credit."

"I'll pay for it, Mr. Heath," the Reverend said hastily. "Let him have what he wants."

Heath gave him an odd look, but nodded. "Looks like we got a deal," he said to Henry.

The Reverend came over with his hand out. "I'm Leland Drury."

Henry shook it. Henry Casey."

"I couldn't help but overhear," Reverend Drury said. "I go to the village often. Their suffering is hard to ignore."

Henry nodded, agreeing.

"I have mules that know the way," Reverend Drury suggested, "if you'd like to use one."

"Well, yeah," Henry said. "Thanks."

Reverend Drury shrugged. "You'd be saving me a trip." He started out of the store, then paused. "Mr. Casey? When was the last time you tasted lamb?"

Henry thought briefly, then shook his head. He and White Fang had eaten fish and potatoes *most* of the time. "Couldn't tell you."

"Come to dinner this evening," Reverend Drury said, with his oily smile. "Seven o'clock."

Henry nodded enthusiastically. "I'll be there."

Reverend Drury nodded back, and left.

"Walks like a soldier," Henry observed.

"Protestant," Adam John said disparagingly.

Reverend Drury's house turned out to be decorated with an elaborate collection of Haida art. The walls were covered with wooden masks, copper shields, and other artifacts. But the only thing Henry could look at was the table covered with steaming dishes of greens, potatoes, and a huge leg of lamb.

Hungrier than he could remember ever being, he ate several servings.

Reverend Drury came behind him with a bottle of wine. "I've been trying for almost a year to get Moses to move off that land," he said. "More wine, Henry?"

"Don't mind if I do . . . Leland," Henry said, and wiped his mouth with the back of his hand. He felt very full, slightly giddy — and altogether cheerful. "But, you know the land's all they got."

Reverend Drury refilled his glass. "You've talked to Moses, then."

Henry nodded. "He's a smart man."

Reverend Drury sat down, his face hard to read. "Reverend Michael thought so."

"Who's that?" Henry asked curiously, helping himself to just *one* more slice of lamb.

Reverend Drury looked startled. "Moses didn't tell you?"

Henry shook his head.

"That's surprising," Reverend Drury said, pouring himself some more wine. "They spent a lot of time together." He set the bottle back on the table. "Reverend Michael was pastor here before me. He disappeared. Strange tale. From what I've gathered, the poor devil got caught up in their madness." He paused for effect. "He left the village one day and went up on Devil's Thumb, looking for the missing hunters. He was never seen again."

That got Henry's full attention, and he listened more closely.

Reverend Drury picked up the carving knife and sliced some more meat. "The Haidas are very primitive, Henry. They don't think like us." He laid a slab of lamb on Henry's plate. "Know what I'd do if I were you?"

Henry shook his head.

"I'd forget about going back out there," Reverend Drury said, looking at him intensely. "I'd take that mule and those supplies, and I'd head on back to that claim of yours and get to work. You can't go back home empty-handed, can you?"

Henry frowned at him, unsure of what he had just heard.

"I'll stake you, Henry," Reverend Drury said. "I know you're good for the money."

Uneasily, Henry put his fork down and pushed his plate to one side. "What about the Haidas?"

"I'll take care of them," Reverend Drury assured him. "And don't worry — it's easier on them if I'm the only one they deal with. Less confusion."

Henry wasn't sure what to say, especially since the idea of going back to his cabin was very tempting. "Well, I don't know . . ."

"I do," Reverend Drury said firmly. "Trust me, Henry. Don't go out there. Don't undo the work I've already done."

Henry didn't say yes or no, but he could tell that the Reverend wasn't looking for an answer. What he had just said had been a command.

Now Henry had to decide if he was going to obey it.

White Fang moved through the darkness behind the village houses, searching for some sign of Henry. A woman left the Wolf House and the wolf froze, watching as she entered another dwelling. Then, giving up, he turned and wandered back up into the hills. He had been so sure that he was going to find Henry somewhere among that tribe, and now he was bitterly disappointed.

He found a spot with a view of the village and dug at the ground with his front paws, creating a hole to block off the cold night air. He curled up in the dirt, but after a minute or two he sat up restlessly and started howling. The howl was a lonely, haunting cry that would have touched the hardest soul.

The wolf pack heard his cry from their night resting place further along the mountainside and stirred from their sleep, listening. Cinnamon, moved by his passion, rose up on her haunches and added her howl to his, forming a sad duet.

Gradually, all of the wolves, from the black leader on down to the cubs, joined in, filling the night air with their plaintive song.

No one down in the village was going to get much sleep tonight.

Chapter 14

In the morning, Henry let Adam John help him load food and supplies into two baskets strapped to a mule. Adam John, closing one of the baskets, noticed something inside. He pulled out a package and unwrapped it to see a lace shawl.

"Who's this for?" he asked, holding it up.

"It's not for *you*," Henry said, blushing a little and snatching it back.

Carefully, he rewrapped the package and put it away. Then, grabbing the mule's halter, he led the reluctant animal down the path.

Adam John picked up his mail satchel and jumped on his bike, riding ahead to show Henry the way.

They stopped at the river, and Adam John looked back at the mining camp in disgust.

"Over a thousand years we've lived on this land," he said. "Soon you will not know we were here. Look already what the white man leaves behind."

Henry nodded, staring back at the ramshackle town. It was a blight on the beautiful landscape.

"Wish you were coming with me," he said.

Adam John climbed onto his bike. "The mail must go through," he said, slapping his satchel. Then, he looked more serious. "They believe in you, Henry. Now — *you* have to believe. You are who they think you are — the White Wolf."

Henry smiled valiantly, and Adam John waved and pedaled off downstream. Henry watched him go before turning and leading the mule upstream.

He didn't notice it, but a raven was flying above him, going his way.

He and the mule trudged endlessly

through the wilderness, the mule giving him more trouble than cooperation.

"Come on!" Henry said, struggling to pull the halter. "Move it, you lazy old bag of bones!"

The mule brayed and planted its hooves, staying right where it was.

"Fine," Henry said and dropped to his knees to catch his breath. He was too tired to go any further, anyway.

Suddenly, a chill ran up the back of his neck. Feeling as though he was being watched, he slowly looked around at the quiet forest. He didn't see anyone, but just in case, he got up and yanked at the mule's halter.

"Come on,' he said. "Let's go."

To his relief, the mule followed.

After a few more hours of walking, they stopped again. The mule nibbled at some green shoots poking up through the ground while Henry sat on a rock, eating some fried fish.

Once again, the clammy feeling of being watched ran up his spine and he scanned the endless horizon with nervous eyes.

He *seemed* to be alone, but he just wasn't sure.

*   *   *

In the underbrush fifty yards away,
Heath, the man from the general store,
pushed back farther into the bushes. The
boy was suspicious, and Heath was under
orders not to be seen.

He saw Henry get up again and encour-
age the mule to start walking.

Heath would be right behind them the
whole way.

Henry was exhausted from climbing hills
by the time he finally saw the village.

"Well, Henry, like they say," he said
aloud. "Follow your heart." He sighed, and
started leading the mule down the hill.

Lily was working at a loom strung from
a tree branch. She looked like an angel fin-
gering a harp. She heard a noise and saw
Henry coming out of the forest, looking exhausted as he pulled the mule.

Skeptical, Lily continued her weaving,
and what few villagers were out and about
at this time of day paid Henry little
attention.

He couldn't help feeling disappointed,
having expected more of a reception, but

he just tied up the mule and started to un-
load his supplies.

Kat'rin came out of the Wolf House, smiling when she saw him.

"You ran away last night," she said. "I
would have fed you."

"But — I just got here," Henry said.

Kat'rin smiled and kept walking.

Henry looked over at Lily. "Where's
Moses?"

"Inside," she said without looking up
from what she was doing. "He's expecting
you."

Henry frowned. "He *is?*"

Lily nodded tightly.

Henry checked to make sure the mule
was tied securely and then turned to go into
the Wolf House.

"Why did you come back?" Lily asked.

Henry stopped. "Isn't that what you
wanted?"

She didn't say anything, looking an-
noyed.

Henry was baffled by her reaction, but
he decided to go for broke, pulling the lace
shawl out from underneath his shirt and
smoothing away the wrinkles.

"This is for you." he said, handing it to her awkwardly.

She made a strange face, but slowly unfurled the shawl, and looked it over.

"Why would I wear this?" she asked, lowering it.

Henry flushed, stung by her rejection. "Uh, I don't know. I — thought it would look pretty."

"Pretty like 'white girl'?" Lily asked.

"*No*," Henry said, starting to lose his temper. "Tell you what — don't wear it. See if I care. Here, give it back!" He grabbed for the shawl, balled it up, and heaved it into the mud.

They glared at each other, both disgusted.

"What do I have to do, anyway?" he asked. "I mean, I came back, didn't I?"

Lily shrugged. "I don't believe you."

"Don't believe what?" he asked.

She looked at him, unblinking. "That your heart is in the right place."

Henry shook his head, completely fed up. "Look, I'm *here*. I came back to help, and I'm going to try to find those caribou, whether you believe me or not. Maybe one of these days, before it's all over, you'll see

I'm not the worthless scum that you think I am."

He was about to storm off when the sound of Moses' voice stopped him.

"Henry Casey," Moses said, from the entryway of the Wolf House. Strangely, he didn't look at all surprised to see him.

Henry nodded, in no mood for conversation as he scowled at Lily's turned back.

"He was here looking for you," Moses said.

"Who was?" Henry asked grumpily.

"The wolf," Moses said.

Henry was going to nod impatiently, but then realized what that might mean. "You mean, White Fang?" he asked hopefully. "He's alive?"

Moses nodded.

Overjoyed, Henry looked at Lily. "Are you sure it was him?"

"Yes," she said. "It was the same wolf."

Henry grinned broadly, the news making him feel better than he had in days.

White Fang was alive!

Chapter 15

At first, Henry was too excited to speak, but then he was full of questions.

"Where is he?" he asked. "Where did he go? How can I find him?"

"Be patient," Moses said. "He'll find you. First, we must prepare you for the hunt. In four days, the moon will be full. There is so much for you to learn." He shook his head ruefully. "So little time, so little time . . ." He turned to his niece. "Lily, go find Kat'rin."

She nodded and ran off.

"Tonight, we do the ceremony," Moses said and walked away, still talking to himself.

Henry just grinned, thinking only about White Fang. Somehow, his wolf had survived!

After trailing Henry to the village, Heath returned to the mining camp and went straight to the church. He entered quietly, closing the door behind him.

Reverend Drury appeared a moment later.

"Well?" he asked.

"He went back to the village," Heath said, wishing that the boy had just gone straight to his claim, instead.

A smile oozed across Reverend Drury's face. "He's an insubordinate young man, isn't he?"

Heath nodded. "Yes, sir, he is."

Reverend Drury nodded, too. "I don't tolerate that, Heath, do I?"

"No, sir," Heath agreed. "You don't."

"No, I don't," Reverend Drury said, and his smile got uglier.

Henry Casey would pay for his disobedience.

That night, the Haidas held a formal hunt ceremony in the Wolf House. Everyone gathered around the fire as drums pulsed in the background.

Two Haida men, with their backs to the group, danced forward in small steps, holding a blanket up at shoulder level between them. With his free hand, each shook a rattle down by his knees. They slowly lowered the blanket to expose Moses, wearing an elaborate wolf mask, complete with a snout that opened and shut.

Moses leaped forward, crouched like the stalking wolf, shuffling his feet as he danced. He didn't move quickly, but rather, in a smooth and deliberate way.

From a dark corner, a Haida man in a caribou mask with real antlers darted out and stopped near Moses. Moses' wolf stalked the caribou as they moved around each other.

At Moses' signal, the drumbeat picked up and he turned towards the entryway as two boys in wolf masks danced their way inside. It was Peter and Henry, Peter leading Henry in the complicated steps.

Peter's dancing was hypnotic as he leaped about, landing on all fours, howling like a wolf. Henry did his best to imitate him, poorly executing the steps as they danced among the villagers. He felt shy in front of their dubious stares and he danced over closer to Moses.

"I shouldn't be out here," he muttered.

"Let the wolf inside you be free," Moses said in a low voice.

Henry moved up and down, studying Peter's actions. Then, bending at the waist with his arms outstretched, he moved behind Moses and Peter as they pursued the caribou in dance.

Then, the howling of a *real* wolf came from outside, somewhere very close to the village. The dancing stopped and everyone inside the Wolf House was very still, listening.

The wolf howled again, long and sorrowful.

Henry yanked off his mask. "That's White Fang!"

"Go," Moses said quickly. "Go!"

Henry handed his mask to Peter and ran outside. He stopped to listen and, when he heard the howl once more, he pulled a firebrand from the fire and used it to light his way as he ran through the woods.

He searched for White Fang, going from tree to tree and waving the firebrand.

Moses and the rest of the villagers poured out of the Wolf House en masse and watched Henry's torch move through the darkness. Moses motioned for everyone else to wait behind and he went to join Henry in the forest.

Henry could feel that an animal was pacing nearby in the darkness, and he paused.

"White Fang?" he called. "White Fang?"

The animal circled around him and Henry knelt down, trying to see into the shadows cast by his flickering light.

"Hey, boy, it's me," he said apprehensively. "Come on!"

Suddenly, the black wolf leaped out and attacked him. Henry threw up his arms and the firebrand was enough to keep the snarling wolf at bay until White Fang dashed out and charged the black wolf.

The fight was short and vicious as White Fang — the stronger of the two — drove the black wolf back into the bushes. Henry listened tensely to a battle he could not see as he waited to find out which of the two wolves would return.

When he heard a wolf's panting breath,

he froze in anticipation. He was either going to be mauled, or see the best friend he had thought was gone forever.

After what seemed like hours, White Fang ran out of the bushes and jumped on him, licking his face exuberantly. The two were finally reunited and Henry buried his head in the wolf's neck, laughing with joy.

"Oh, man, I can't believe it," he said, over and over. "White Fang! White Fang, you're back. I knew you weren't dead. How'd you find me?"

In answer, White Fang jumped up and ran around like a puppy, circling Henry and darting in between trees, his tail beating in a white blur.

Henry smiled at the sight before pulling him back and checking him for injuries.

"Are you all right?" he asked. "Where were you? What happened?"

Cinnamon slunk into the clearing and growled deep in her throat. Henry looked at her, then back at White Fang. White Fang went over to nuzzle her and then returned to Henry, wagging his tail.

"You found a friend, hunh?" Henry said, grinning.

Cinnamon came closer, but jumped back

when she heard Moses calling "Henry! Henry Casey!"

"Be right there," Henry called and started towards him.

White Fang stayed where he was.

"Come on, boy," Henry said.

White Fang hesitated, his loyalties being tested. Then, he went over to join Henry and Cinnamon turned abruptly, melting away into the woods.

She went straight to the beaten black wolf. Together they watched Henry and White Fang leave.

White Fang had found his master — and lost his mate.

Chapter 16

With White Fang by his side, Henry walked with a new confidence.

"Moses!" he said cheerfully, seeing the Chief coming his way.

Moses' tired eyes were playing tricks on him as he looked through the eyeholes of the mask and saw Henry and the wolf seem to meld, to be one and the same.

"The White Wolf," Moses whispered and removed his mask, looking up at the sky. "Thank you. Thank you."

White Fang growled and Henry stroked his head. The wolf instantly quieted.

"Now I understand," Moses said.

They walked back to the village, emerging from the forest like an apparition. The Haidas were struck with awe, seeing that the myth of the White Wolf had come to life. A little hum of wonder ran through the crowd as now, for the first time, they began to believe.

Moses lifted his hands to quiet them.

"The boy and the wolf have become one," he said. "From this time on, Henry Casey is the White Wolf." He said the name "White Wolf" in Haida and the people repeated it three times.

Henry stood there, fully energized, believing, at least for now, that it was true. He was one with the White Wolf.

"When the moon is full, he will hunt the caribou," Moses announced.

Lily stood at the edge of the crowd, her eyes filling with tears as she watched this transpire. She had not failed; she *had* found the White Wolf and brought him back, after all.

When it was time for bed, Henry laid out a blanket in his sleeping area and White Fang walked around in a circle on it before lying down.

"It's good to have you back, boy," Henry

said, patting him. "No matter what happens."

He was wrapping a blanket around himself when he felt someone behind him and saw Lily standing there with an apologetic look on her face. She was holding a set of leathers.

"These belonged to my brother," she said, handing the pair of handmade pants and shirt to him.

He took them shyly.

"I was wrong about you, Henry Casey," she said.

He shrugged self-consciously. "That's okay, Lily."

She beamed at him. "Sleep well — White Wolf," she said. Then she was gone.

Henry sat down, feeling a foolish smile spreading across his own face.

"She *likes* me," he said to White Fang, and smiled some more.

He was awakened the next morning by a burst of sunlight as Moses slid open a roof board above him. Henry opened his eyes, instinctively feeling for White Fang, delighted to find the wolf right there by his side.

Moses smiled down at them. "It begins now, White Wolf."

Henry yawned, pulled on his boots, and he and White Fang headed outside.

He found Moses and Lily standing by a leaping fire. Moses reached into the burning coals, grabbed a hot black stone with his bare hand, and dropped it into a pot. The water boiled instantly.

Henry looked at Lily in astonishment, but she didn't react.

The Chief, using a knife, cut the bark of the Devil's Club plant he had gathered earlier and dropped it into the steaming pot.

"This is Devil's Club juice and salt water," he explained. "For three days, you will fast, perform the rituals, and drink only this."

Henry nodded, a little overwhelmed.

"To hunt is a sacred act," Moses went on. "You must purify your body to be worthy of the kill. Your mind must be clear of all else — no distractions."

Henry gulped, but nodded.

Lily stepped forward to put more wood on the fire, and Henry couldn't help watching her as she returned to the Wolf House. Moses caught him staring.

"You care for Lily?" he asked.

"Yes, sir," Henry said, the words coming straight from his heart. "I do."

"Lily does not yield so easily," Moses said.

Henry nodded. "She's tough, all right."

"All Haida women are like this," Moses agreed, "but Lily learned when she was very young."

"Why's that?" Henry asked.

Moses sighed. "Already, death has visited her three times." He drew his finger across his forearm three times, indicating Lily's scars. "Her mother, her father, her brother — all taken by the smallpox. The white man's plague. So Lily found her strength early."

Henry nodded, saddened by this revelation.

"It is out of your hands, White Wolf. Haida women do the choosing." Moses smiled sadly. "And the sun will set on top of my head before Lily yields. You must put her out of your mind."

"That's not going to be so easy," Henry said, looking at the Wolf House.

Moses scooped out a bowl of the hot Devil's Club juice. "Drink this."

Henry sniffed the bowl, took a sip, and then — with Moses urging him on — drained it.

Instantly, the juice reacted inside his intestines and he jumped to his feet, not sure where to run.

Moses knew the problem and pointed towards the woods.

Henry took off at a full run, already yanking his pants down.

He was starting to get the idea that the next few days were going to be extremely difficult.

Chapter 17

When the bout was over, Henry came back, and on Moses' instructions, he waded out and stood in the cold stream, shivering.

Moses waited on the shore, signaling with his arms for Henry to sit down.

"Faster you sit, faster you get out," he said.

Henry looked down at the uninviting water, his arms wrapped tightly around himself, while White Fang paced at the edge of the water, whining as he watched Henry's discomfort.

Slowly, Henry lowered himself into the icy water. Immediately, his face turned blue and his teeth began to chatter. He stayed in the water as long as he could and then ran to the bank, grabbing a blanket and moving as close to the fire as he could get.

Moses reached up and broke off a branch from a willow tree. "Stand up."

Henry ignored him, and Moses hit his back with the branch. As White Fang growled ominously, Henry jumped up in a fury and dropped the blanket. Moses hit him across the back again . . . and again.

"Warms your blood," he explained.

Henry realized that he wasn't cold anymore, and he smiled. It was time to stop questioning and start trusting whatever the Chief said.

Next they went to a steep rise on the mountain behind the village and Moses told Henry to start running up and down the hill.

Henry did what he was told, White Fang romping next to him. The wolf was having a good time, but Henry wasn't. He collapsed from exhaustion and rolled all the way to the bottom of the hill, and remained where he had landed.

Moses got up from where he had been

sitting in the shade and poured water over him. Henry groaned, and sat up.

"You try too hard," Moses said sternly. "Stop the noise in your head. Watch the wolf. Never hurries. Always steady."

Henry, breathing hard, looked at White Fang.

"Watch him," Moses said. "Learn from him. He sees in the dark, hears sounds before they come. He moves, always searching for clues." He pointed at Henry's chest. "The wolf is in all of us. On the other side, where we all connect, what you don't know will help you, if you let it."

White Fang, who was not even panting, turned and looked at them.

"See the eyes," Moses said. "There is a story that a man once tried to change all the animals into people — and succeeded only in making human the eyes of the wolf." He smiled. "Good story."

Henry tried to smile back and then did his best to stand up, his muscles weak and exhausted.

Moses put his hand out to help him. "When your legs ache, reach inside for the other strength the creator has given you."

"What if it's not there?" Henry asked.

"Look again," Moses said, with a shrug.

Henry nodded, took a deep breath, and forced himself to run back up the hill.

Neither of them saw the long barrel of a rifle peeking out from the bushes and pointing at Henry. Heath was lying there, holding the rifle, and he had a clean shot. He gripped the gun, with sweat pouring down his face and his finger trembling against the trigger.

Then, after a long minute, he lowered the rifle, let the hammer down, and exhaled heavily.

Reverend Drury had ordered him to kill Henry — and he just couldn't do it.

When the Reverend found out, he was going to be very angry.

That night, after his exhausting day of training, Henry staggered into the Wolf House and collapsed on his blankets. He started snoring almost before he had time to close his eyes.

White Fang slipped into the room and curled up next to him, his eyes wide open as he kept watch.

Henry slept like a dead man until the sound of low arguing voices woke him up. He looked out and saw Moses, Peter, and Sshaga, the Holy Man, gathered around the fire pit. He also saw that it was Peter who was arguing, while Moses listened calmly.

"We have the wolf," Peter protested. "Why do we need the boy?"

"They are one and the same," Moses said.

Peter frowned. "In the dream, it was a *wolf*."

"Dreams have many shapes" was Moses' only answer.

Peter started to respond to that, but Moses raised his hand for silence, and Peter closed his mouth obediently.

"I know this is hard for you, son," Moses said. "Be patient. Your time will come."

Peter nodded with resignation and stood up.

"Peter," his father said, thoughtfully. "It's not good to go through the rituals alone."

Peter heard what his father was saying and knew that it wasn't an order, but just a suggestion. He nodded, and left the room without answering.

* * *

The next day, Moses put Henry through the same brutal exercises, as White Fang paced uneasily back and forth. Henry forced himself to drink a bowl of Devil's Club juice, gagging at the taste, and then he dropped his blanket, walked into the cold water, and sat down up to his neck.

Soon the temperature was unbearable and he was about to run out when Peter appeared, wading in next to him.

"Where you going?" Peter asked, and sat down without any hesitation.

Henry shivered, looking longingly at the fire, but lowered himself back down, facing Peter.

"Be still," Peter said. "Don't fight it."

Henry saw how calm the young warrior was, apparently not bothered by the freezing temperatures at all. He did his best to concentrate on not shivering, blocking out the pain with his mind. He held it back for a long minute, impressing even himself.

"Piece of cake," he said confidently.

But speaking broke his concentration and the agony returned, forcing him to jump up and run back to the shore. Instead of sitting by the fire, he made himself pass by the willow tree and tear a branch from it, using the branch to whip himself.

Standing up on the hills above the village and watching this scene, Lily smiled to herself.

Chapter 18

Heath dragged himself back to the mining camp, dreading the conversation he was about to have. He stood at the bottom of the stairs leading to the church, then lowered his head and started up the steps.

Reverend Drury was waiting for him. "Well, Mr. Heath?"

Heath ducked his head guiltily. "He was still at the village."

"*And?*" Reverend Drury said pointedly.

Heath sighed, unable to meet his gaze. "He's only a boy, Leland."

"That *boy* could ruin everything!" Reverend Drury shouted, then shook his head angrily. "Do I have to do *everything* myself?"

Heath shrugged, and looked guilty.

Back in the village, Henry stood by the stream, practicing his archery. He drew back his bow and sent an arrow flying towards a target painted on the trunk of a massive fir tree.

The arrow missed the tree completely and sailed into the woods.

"Stop the noise," Henry told himself. "Stop the noise in your head."

He notched another arrow, drew the bow, and let it fly. This time, the arrow missed the target, but *did* hit the tree trunk.

Out of nowhere, another arrow sliced through the air and hit the target dead center.

Henry looked around, but didn't see anyone.

"Nice shot!" he said to the unknown archer.

Once again, he pulled back on his bow, but before his arrow even got close to the tree, yet another phantom arrow hit the target right in the middle.

"Is that you, Moses?" Henry called.

There was a sound something like a crow's caw, and then quiet muffled laughter.

White Fang realized who it was, and barked. Hiding behind a tree, Lily smiled mischievously and put her finger to her lips to quiet him.

"Peter?!" Henry yelled, and then jumped back as another arrow plunged into the ground at his feet. "Hey! What the — "

Lily stepped out from behind the tree and Henry stared at her, his mouth agape.

"That was *you?*" he said.

She retrieved her arrow casually. "You don't believe a woman can shoot?"

"I do now," Henry said.

Lily nodded, and looked him over. "I can teach you."

"Uh, okay," Henry said uncertainly.

"But you must do what I say." She came up behind him, placing her hand over his on the bow and notching an arrow.

They were standing very close and both felt the heat from each other's bodies as they drew the bow back together.

"No thoughts," Lily whispered. "There

122

is nothing else in the world but you, this arrow, and the tree."

Henry swallowed, trying to concentrate.

"And you are all *one*," she said, gently letting his hands go. "Now let it fly."

He released the arrow and it hit the target — not a bull's-eye, but close enough. He turned to smile at her, both of them flushed with pleasure, but then they became aware of how close they were and each took a step back.

"Okay," Lily said, her voice a little unsteady. "Try again."

Later Henry, Peter, and White Fang ran up and down the steep hillside under Moses' watchful eye. Peter pushed Henry, forcing him to climb higher and higher, and then raced him to the bottom.

On their way back up, their legs pumping furiously, Peter noticed Henry glancing at Lily as she passed by.

"Where you come from," he demanded, "there are no women?"

Henry grinned.

"We never see them," Peter said. "Always only men."

"No, no, there's women," Henry said. "Beautiful women. They're just too soft for living up here."

Peter frowned at him. "So you want Haida girl?"

"I want Lily," Henry said.

"But Lily's a princess," Peter said.

Henry shrugged, running harder. "I don't care."

Peter shook his head with dismay, and they kept running, up, down, and back up again.

"We don't buy presents," Peter said, out of breath. "If you want to tell Haida girl you care for her, you come up behind her, put your chin on her shoulder and talk softly in her ear."

Henry looked over. "That's it? She'll understand?"

Peter nodded. "Or break your nose."

They both laughed.

"You don't choose Haida woman," Peter said. "She chooses you."

Henry nodded, taking in his words, and they kept running.

At the end of the day, Moses summoned Henry to the fire pit inside the Wolf House. There, he handed him something in a leather case, while Peter looked on, crushed.

"Grandfather's bow," Lily said softly.

Henry opened the case, finding an old black yew-wood bow and a quiver of white arrows. He shook his head and handed it back. "I can't take this."

"You will need it," Moses said.

Henry accepted it reluctantly, aware of Peter's and Lily's eyes burning into the back of his head. When he looked at them, Peter walked out, and he looked back at Moses.

"Let them come with me," he said.

Moses frowned. "Women do not hunt."

"Why?" Henry asked.

"Old ways," Lily said grimly, and went to her sleeping area, where she sat down to listen.

"But, Peter," Henry said. "Can't he go? He's ready. *I'm* not — and you know it."

Moses looked off in the distance, thinking.

"I know the mountain is sacred," Henry said. "I respect that, sir, I do. But if *I* can go, maybe they can make another exception."

There was a long silence.

"I will ask the Holy Man," Moses said finally.

He went, alone, to the Holy Man's hut. It was set off by itself, with a frog totem pole on the roof, and heavy smoke seeping out through the wall boards, day and night. Moses spoke to the shaman in Haida, and then slowly walked outside, coughing from the smoke, deeply disturbed by the oracle's response.

Lily, Peter, and Kat'rin were all waiting for him just outside the shack.

Moses stared into his son's eager eyes. "You can go on the mountain," he said. "You can hunt."

Peter tried to control his excitement but couldn't, letting out a triumphant yelp. As he ran off, the rest of them walked back towards the Wolf House.

"In the pack, it is the female wolf who runs down the caribou," Lily ventured.

Her uncle frowned at her. "Lily, you can't go. Now, stop. My head aches."

"But I am better than Peter with the bow," Lily protested. "You know this. Besides, who found the White Wolf?"

"He found you," Moses said shortly.

Lily gave up, and walked ahead of them

without further argument, her shoulders slumped with disappointment.

Kat'rin looked up at Moses, aware of the deep sadness in his eyes. "What else did he see?" she asked.

Moses looked at her unhappily. "One of them will not return," he said.

Chapter 19

Henry stood in the Wolf House, trying to practice with the black yew bow. He pulled back the string, fired an arrow at a post — and missed. The arrow ricocheted off walls, zipped past White Fang, and stuck in a board next to Henry's head.

Distressed, he looked at White Fang. "What am I *doing*, boy?" he asked, shaking his head.

Moses appeared unexpectedly in the doorway.

"Peter will hunt with you," he said.

"Great!" Henry answered, and then realized from Moses' expression that he should tone down his enthusiasm a little. "I mean, good."

Moses nodded, his eyes dark and sad. "Sleep well, White Wolf. You will need it."

Henry lay back on his blanket, elated by what he had just been told. He felt a lot better knowing that he and White Fang would not be going out there into the wilderness alone.

Early the next morning, Reverend Drury kicked his way into the general store and stumbled inside. He had been up all night and was very drunk.

Heath came out in his long johns.

"Get dressed, you pig," Reverend Drury said. He went behind the counter, broke into a locked cabinet, and helped himself to some ammunition. He took out a pistol and began clumsily loading it.

"What for?" Heath asked.

Reverend Drury shoved the loaded pistol into his pocket. "We're going to the village," he said.

Right after she woke up, Lily brought her lace shawl down to the water and tried to wash out the mud stains without success. Finally, she threw the shawl down in frustration.

Kat'rin came over and picked it up, studying the stains, also shaking her head.

Lily watched her work at the stains until she saw Henry and White Fang come out of the Wolf House to join Peter, who had been waiting for them. The boys walked over to the water, dropped their blankets, strolled out, and sat down up to their necks.

The last day of the rituals had begun.

Minutes passed as the two boys sat in the water, eyeing each other like blue-skinned gunfighters.

"Don't hurt yourself," Peter said.

Henry shrugged. "This is a little warm for me."

Peter, who was feeling the pain, was amazed by Henry's threshold. They stared at each other, and Peter was unable to see the quit in Henry's eyes.

"We leave together," he suggested.

"On three," Henry said, and then counted slowly. "One . . . two . . . three!"

Neither boy moved; neither of them had ever planned to move. These moments of extreme hardship had cemented a friendship between them and they smiled at each other.

"You are crazy, White Wolf," Peter said. "Good crazy." He stood up, exhaled, and walked out of the water.

Henry exploded from the water, caught up to him, and they walked to the shore together to get their willow branches and restore their circulation.

Later, Moses took Henry out to the hills, below the mountain known as Devil's Thumb. Moses bobbed his head confidently as he looked at White Fang.

"He brought us here. This is a good sign." He pointed up at the mountain. "You go up beyond the old village. There you will find a trail to take you onto the mountain."

Henry nodded thoughtfully, and they both looked up at the forbidding mountain.

"I know a fish that wants to be eaten," Moses said, breaking the silence. "This way."

They went to a stream where Moses squatted down and submerged his hands in the water as he stared down at them.

"Moses?" Henry asked shyly. "What if I still don't believe?"

"Trust me," Moses said. "It will all become clear."

It was still hard for Henry to trust blindly. "But — "

"Shhh," Moses said, without moving a muscle. Then he lunged forward, pulling out a wriggling fifteen-inch trout with his hands.

Henry stared at the fish, flabbergasted. "How'd you do that?"

"My father taught me," Moses said, and he snapped the trout's neck expertly. He tore off the head and, using his knife with the dexterity of a surgeon, carved out the fish's cheeks. He ate one and offered the other to Henry.

Henry ate the raw fish, surprised to find himself enjoying the taste. As he swallowed, something over Moses' shoulder caught his eye, and he turned pale.

Moses caught the terror in Henry's eyes and turned very slowly to see what was the matter.

Twenty yards away, a huge brown bear was waddling to the water's edge for a drink.

Henry was about to bolt, but Moses stopped him with soft words, trying not to alarm him further.

"Don't move," he said.

Henry stayed stock-still, not sure how Moses could be so relaxed.

"You run, he'll get one of us," Moses said.

Smelling the fish, the bear turned and looked at them.

"He sees us," Henry said, barely able to control his panic. "He sees us!"

"Do you want to die?" Moses asked.

The bear stood up and sniffed the air. He was nine feet tall, weighed over nine hundred pounds, and had a monstrous head.

"Moses," Henry started shakily.

"He smells your fear," Moses said, his voice quietly sharp. "Be still. Breathe deep."

The bear dropped down on all fours and charged for them, but stopped when they didn't react.

"Here he comes," Moses said, his lips barely moving. "Don't think. Clear your mind, White Wolf. Control your fear."

Henry fought every impulse he had to run, trying not to tremble visibly.

"Don't be afraid," Moses said in a soothing voice. "He doesn't want to hurt us. He's not hungry. There's plenty of fish."

The bear circled slowly, watching them as he waded past in the water. He stopped, and they were face to face.

Racked with fear, Henry averted his eyes.

"No," Moses said. "Look at him."

Henry struggled to overcome the wrenching terror that wanted to take his body in another direction, and met the bear's cross-eyed gaze.

"He's just a big cub," Moses said. "More afraid of you than you are of him."

Henry's breathing slowed down and a noticeable calm settled over him. His muscles relaxed and he boldly stared into the bear's eyes, his fear in check.

"See?" Moses said as the bear moved closer. "He likes you."

The contrast in size between them and the bear was staggering and they sat like rocks, neither breathing nor blinking. The bear was inches away from them and when his leg brushed across Henry's face, Henry remained calm.

"I know what he wants," Moses said.

The bear delicately reached between them and snatched up the fish. He sat back in the water and, holding it in his paws, devoured the fish, leaving only the head and spine.

"I guess he was hungry," Moses said.

The bear rose to his full height and looked at something behind them. Then, feeling no challenge, he dropped down, and splashed away through the water and crashed off into the woods.

Moses looked over his shoulder and saw White Fang standing some distance away like a sentinel.

Henry was just coming out of his trance, looking like a different person, and he turned accepting eyes on Moses, waiting for his next test.

"You looked death in the eyes, and you were not there. You were invisible," Moses said, and smiled. "Now you are ready."

Chapter 20

When they returned to the village, they found Sshaga watching as Reverend Drury rode up on his powerful stallion.

"Morning, Moses," he said drily. "Walk with me, Henry. We have to talk."

Something in his manner made Henry hesitate.

Reverend Drury put on a smile. "I've got good news."

"Yeah?" Henry said, hanging back. "What's that?"

"A friend of mine is shipping a load of gold to Fort Tongass," Reverend Drury said, swinging down off the horse. "He needs a man he can trust to get it there. It pays a thousand dollars."

Henry had no response.

"It would pay your way home and then some," Reverend Drury said, "but you'd have to leave today."

Henry shook his head. "I can't do that. I gave Moses my word."

"Tomorrow, White Wolf will lead a hunt to Devil's Thumb," Moses said proudly.

Reverend Drury looked confused. "White Wolf?"

Moses smiled, and gestured towards Henry. "Henry Casey."

Now the Reverend looked incensed and he glared at Henry, who just shrugged. Reverend Drury grabbed his arm and pulled him away.

"I'm losing my patience, Henry," he said. "These people may think you're something special, but I know you're not. I'm warning you. *Don't* go up on that mountain."

"*Warning* me?" Henry said, mimicking his furious inflections. "What kind of religion *are* you?"

Reverend Drury lowered his voice. "Same as you, boy."

Henry backed away from him. "I don't know who you are — or what you want with these people — but I know it isn't right. So pack up and get out of here."

"Don't show off at my expense," Reverend Drury answered. "It'll come back to haunt you."

Henry leaned over and gave him a hard shove in the chest. "I said, go on! Get out of here!"

Reverend Drury's hand snaked inside his coat, and then, after a tense moment, he pulled out a Bible.

"I'll pray for you," he said, and he climbed back on his horse.

He rode out to the forest where Heath, also on horseback, was waiting for him.

"Tell them to get ready," Reverend Drury ordered. "I'll be out there as soon as I can."

Heath nodded, and kicked his horse into a swift canter to go tell the others.

That night, Henry couldn't sleep. He tossed and turned for a while, then got up. He walked outside among the totem poles, whistling and calling for White Fang. When the wolf didn't come, he sat down, looking up at the magnificent moonlit pole looming above him.

Lily came out of the darkness and stood nearby.

"My grandfather's pole," she said. "It tells of a great Haida Chief. Bear clan. His father, the Wolf. Mother, Calm Woman with Fish. Raven — my father." She let out her breath. "To be remembered by a pole is a great honor."

Henry got up and stood next to her.

"In my clan, there have been many chiefs and warrior women," Lily went on. "They are part of who I am. I carry all of them with me — the dead — the living — even the ones yet to be born. And they carry me. We belong only to each other." She looked seriously at him. "That is the way it is, and they can never take that from us. Do you understand?"

Henry nodded. "Since I've been here, I've even felt that way, myself."

She looked at him quizzically.

Henry stopped, groping for the right words. "You know — a part of something. I've never felt more at home, anywhere."

"When all of this is done," Lily said, sounding tentative, "and you go back to your world, I hope you will not forget."

"I'll *never* forget you," Henry said quietly.

"And I won't forget you, White Wolf." Lily smiled. "The river delivered you at my feet."

Henry looked at her, aching to hold her. "Lily, there has to be a way — "

She shook her head at the enormity and impossibility of it.

"What do I have to do?" he asked. "Tell me. I'll do it."

"It's not possible," Lily said.

He sighed. "But I want to be with you."

Lily shook her head firmly, moving away from him. "Don't talk like that."

Henry came right after her. "I want us to be together."

"I am Lily Joseph," she said stubbornly. "My grandfather was a chief. I will marry one of my own."

"I want to stay here, make this my home," Henry insisted. "I want to learn your language. Lily, I want to be *part* of this with you."

Lily shook her head, looking cynical. "That will change."

"No, it won't," Henry said.

"*You'll* change," Lily said.

If he wasn't sure of anything else, Henry *was* sure of this. "I'm not going to change how I feel about you."

Lily wanted to believe him, but she turned away. "You'll leave. It's not possible."

He came up behind her, gently placed his head on her shoulder, and spoke in a whisper. "Lily."

She shook her head. "No."

"Lily." He reached out and clasped her arms. "Please . . ."

"But, it's not . . ." She stopped and looked into his eyes, and saw the truth of his love for her. ". . . possible," she finished weakly.

"Believe me," Henry said. He drew her into his arms.

Their lips brushed together, but the contact was too much for her and she fled, leaving Henry standing alone under the stars, still able to feel her lips on his.

He was elated — and miserable.

Chapter 21

In the morning, Henry woke up to find White Fang lying alertly beside him and Lily waiting out by his doorway. He smiled sleepily at both of them.

"I brought you food," Lily said.

Henry took the bowl and ate, trying to think of what to say to her.

"Lily," he bagan, "I — "

"You were in my dreams," she admitted. "But there it must stop."

This was his first meal in four days, but he lost his appetite, anyway. "Why?"

"Because of who I am — and who you are," she said. "And that is the way it is."

Behind them, Kat'rin was building up the

morning fire and Lily quickly moved to help her. Henry sighed and picked up Moses' black bow, studying it while he contemplated what lay ahead.

"Are you ready, White Wolf?" Moses asked when Henry went outside.

Henry nodded.

"All right." Moses pointed to a spot on the ground a few feet away and handed him an eagle feather. "If you are in balance, White Wolf, you will hit that spot."

Henry took a deep breath and threw the feather, hitting the spot right in the middle.

"Very well," Moses said. "We must prepare."

Sshaga came and wiped down Henry, White Fang, and Peter with the traditional water and muskeg moss. In the meantime, the villagers readied the boys' weapons, gear, and food, and Kat'rin painted one red line under White Fang's eyes.

"It has begun," Moses said solemnly. "Walk fast. I hear the caribou coming."

Henry saw Kat'rin and the other villagers making preparations of their own, now that the boys were packed.

"Where are they going?" he asked.

"We follow soon behind you," Moses explained. "We care for the wounded. Bring home the dead."

That wasn't exactly what Henry had wanted to hear, but he appreciated the thought. He looked at the villagers, feeling proud to be one of them.

Before they left, he saw Lily standing away from the group, looking disappointed. He went over to her, and took her arm.

"I didn't make these rules," he said. "If I could take you with me, I would. You know that."

She nodded, believing him. "Return safely, White Wolf."

"Lily, don't give up on us. I'll be back," he promised.

They looked into each other's eyes, feeling mutual love, but there were too many people around. So, Henry turned away and went to catch up with Peter and White Fang.

Lily watched him go, gently holding the spot on her arm where he had touched her, wishing with all her heart that she was going along.

She went to her sleeping area and flopped down in the darkness, staring angrily up at the ceiling. It really wasn't fair of Moses to make her stay home. Henry and Peter *needed* her.

Then, feeling something underneath her, she reached down, and found Moses' black bow hidden beneath her blanket.

Lily looked at the bow, then got up, knowing what she had to do.

Once Henry and Peter had left the village, White Fang raced ahead of the boys and into the forest, having caught the scent of the pack. He led the wolves down to the river, dove in, and swam across.

Unfortunately, Cinnamon and the pack didn't follow him. White Fang stood on the other side, hoping that they would join him, but the black wolf scratched fiercely at the ground, then turned and led the pack away.

Cinnamon lingered behind for a minute, but then joined the others.

White Fang was disappointed, but he wheeled around and chased after Henry and Peter. Where they were going, they were going to need him.

Henry and Peter ate on the run, aware that there was no time to waste. Afraid that they were being followed, Henry looked back anxiously, but saw nothing unusual.

Peter tapped on his shoulder, and pointed at White Fang, who was running along parallel to them.

Henry smiled, greatly relieved. They *were* being followed.

"Are you prepared to die?" Peter asked.

Henry shook his head. "Nobody's going to die."

"You must be ready," Peter said seriously. "When I die, I will come back as a Raven and live in the forest behind the village." He paused. "And make so much noise that no one will *ever* sleep." He leaped into the air, his arms flapping like a bird, and they laughed together.

Then it was quiet again, except for the wind rustling through the trees.

"I'm scared," Peter said.

Henry nodded, taking some comfort in that. "So am I."

Peter also looked as though that admission made him feel better. "I had many reasons not to respect you, White Wolf," he said. "Now I have none."

Henry looked at him, amazed that they

had become such good friends. Peter had changed from someone he disliked into someone he couldn't imagine being without. He had never had a brother, and now he felt as though he did. It felt *good*.

When they got to the forest at the base of the mountain they walked more slowly, dwarfed by the canopy of giant spruce trees above them. They were passing the area where the old village had been located — before the earth shook and sent half the mountain down on top of it.

Few walls remained to show evidence of previous Haida dwellings, but the sad faces of crumbling totem poles peeked up from overgrown moss. Broken burial platforms surrounded them.

Henry and Peter walked slowly, and respectfully, not wanting to disturb the dead.

Ahead of them, White Fang started up the path that wound along the side of the mountain at a steep angle. There was a granite wall on one side and a sheer drop-off on the other.

Hesitantly, the boys followed the wolf.

"Caribou make this trail," Peter said.

Henry indicated some tracks on the ground. "Caribou on horseback?"

Peter bent to examine the tracks, his face troubled. There was a low moaning sound and he looked even more worried.

"The dead talking," he said.

Henry swallowed, not wanting to believe it.

In front of them, White Fang suddenly stopped and Peter slowed Henry, who hadn't noticed. They paused just in the nick of time as a six-foot log suspended from the end of a rope swung down from the trees in a pendulum arc and slammed against the rock wall.

Henry and Peter looked at each other. If they hadn't stopped in time, they would have been crushed.

"White man's tricks," Henry said.

Peter nodded, and they continued forward, more alert than ever.

White Fang went around a bend, walking three paces ahead of them. In mid-stride he felt the earth below him give way. The wolf sprang up into the air like a deer and landed on the other side of a gaping pit. Then he turned, waiting for the boys.

Henry and Peter looked down into the pit and saw that the bottom was studded with spikes to impale its unlucky captive.

They both shivered and then took running starts, leaping safely to the other side.

They exchanged glances again — and kept going, climbing bravely and doggedly up the mountain. The wind was picking up, and they saw a wolf carcass hanging from a rope above them.

The sight scared Henry and he retreated, flattening against the rock wall, too spooked to go on.

"I will cut it down," Peter said and went towards the tree.

Henry tried to stop him. "Not now, Peter."

Behind them a raven flew out of the trees, and then they heard the whine and thud of something powerful taking out chunks of wood, tearing out holes in the earth around them.

"What is it?" Peter yelled.

It was a rifle — and someone was firing at them.

Chapter 22

White Fang saw the red flash from the rifle barrel concealed in the rocky crags above them and jumped at Henry, knocking him down out of the way. Staying low, Henry scuttled over and dragged Peter behind some small boulders, out of danger.

"What's happening?" Peter asked.

Henry stuck his head out, and a shot hit the rock right next to him. Swiftly, he ducked back.

"It's gunfire, but — I can't tell where it's coming from," he said, panting.

When more shots hit, they looked behind them, considering that possible exit, only to see a man on horseback coming up the pass, whacking at the brush with a shining saber.

They were trapped.

"I could always outrun a horse," Peter said, trying to keep his voice steady.

Henry shook his head, grabbing Peter's arm to keep him from leaving. "No."

Peter thought for minute, then knocked Henry's hand away, and leaped to his feet.

"Find the caribou," he said, and he took off.

"Peter!" Henry shouted, even though it was too late.

Peter ran, drawing the gunner's fire as more bullets ripped at the earth by his feet. The horseman saw him and also gave chase, as Henry watched in horror.

The last he saw of his friend was Peter racing over the rise, drawing the gunfire and leading their enemies away from Henry and White Fang.

And then he was gone.

At first Henry was too stunned to move, but then he began to shake as the awful moaning of the dead grew louder. He held White Fang tightly against him, taking deep breaths and trying to calm down.

There were two paths in front of him,

and he had to take one. While he was deciding, White Fang bolted out to the left and two shots followed him up the hill. Henry took that as a bad omen and ran the other way.

He thought he had made the safe choice when, out of nowhere, he stepped into a leather snare trap. A heavy tree branch sprang free and he was jerked up off the ground and left hanging upside down. Disoriented, and feeling like a fool, he swayed in the breeze, struggling to get loose.

On a plateau halfway up the mountain, seated behind a large wooden crate, with his finger on the trigger of a rifle, the man with the gun smiled broadly. Henry was swinging as temptingly as a target in a shooting gallery.

The gunner was about to squeeze the trigger when a flaming arrow suddenly rocketed towards him and lodged inside his crate. The gunner dropped his gun and ran away as the crate burst into flames and the rifle exploded, shells popping everywhere.

Down on the hillside, Lily lowered Moses' black bow and went to help Henry get down from the tree.

When he saw her heading towards him

with White Fang, he couldn't believe his eyes.

"You see?" she said. "Women *do* hunt."

Henry did his best to look innocent. "You mean I didn't leave that bow behind by accident?"

Lily smiled and pulled out her knife. "Hold onto me," she said.

Henry put his arms around her as she reached up and cut the leather thong. He dropped to the ground, knocking them both over, and they ended up with their legs tangled.

For a few seconds, they just smiled. Then Lily returned to reality.

"Where's Peter?" she asked.

Henry pointed. "He ran off that way."

Lily looked in that direction, concerned.

Henry stood up, brushing himself off. "Lily, you go back. Get help."

"No," she said, shaking her head. "We stay together."

Another shot thudded nearby and White Fang started running up the hill.

"I'm staying with him," Henry said.

Lily nodded and they hurried up the hill after the wolf, the moaning of the dead loud around them. They followed White Fang up the side of the mountain until he rounded a bend and went out of sight.

Hearing his bark, they climbed up to see what he had found, the moaning now deafening in its intensity. When they rounded the bend, they saw White Fang standing at the edge of the same cliff that Henry and Moses had seen in their dreams.

Henry and Lily pushed past the wolf, and stared down into a narrow canyon at a herd of caribou. They were running, only to find that the pass that led to the other side was blocked by a wall of stones.

Some of the caribou turned to go back the way they had come, but most reached the wall and panicked, getting trapped by the rest of the herd coming in behind them. As they rubbed up against the sides of the canyon, trying to escape, their sad, baying cries echoed off the glacier, creating the moaning sound.

"Holy mackerel!" Henry whispered. He patted White Fang. "You found them, boy! Just like Moses said."

"Just like in the dream!" Lily said excitedly.

White Fang started making his way down the rise and they followed him. Loose glacier stones made the footing very treacherous.

Lily slipped and fell and Henry grabbed her hand, trying to stop her. Instead, he just got pulled right along with her and they crashed into a huge hole overgrown with tree roots and grass.

White Fang ran to the edge of the hole, barking anxiously, not sure what had happened to them.

The hole led to a tunnel and Henry and Lily toppled into it, sliding down and landing in a pile top of each other. The low moaning sound was gone, but they could still hear White Fang's frantic barks.

Henry fumbled in his pockets for a match and lit it.

"Where are we?" Lily asked uneasily.

Henry held out the match and saw an elbow of the tunnel leading off into darkness. "Looks like the air shaft of a mine. Come on."

They crawled into the main tunnel and stood up. Henry's match had burned out and he struck another so that they could see where they were.

They were in the middle of a gold mine, surrounded by piles of ore!

Chapter 23

"Wow!" Henry said, looking around at the vast fortune in gold.

"Is that what I think it is?" Lily asked, having never been inside a mine before.

"Your family know this is here?" Henry asked.

She shook her head.

"This is a gold mine, Lily," he said, speaking both literally and metaphorically. "Know what that means?"

Lily nodded. "Money."

"Lots of money," Henry agreed. "That's why they want to keep you away from here."

They heard voices and pulled back near the air shaft, hiding.

"We have to get out of here," Henry whispered. "Get some help."

"But the caribou will turn around and not come back," Lily said.

Henry shrugged, pulling himself up into the air shaft. "We can't help that."

"We need to knock down that wall," Lily said, with her usual determination.

Henry looked at her doubtfully. "We'd need dynamite."

"Miners have dynamite," she said, smiling.

Realizing what she meant, Henry shook his head. It was much too risky. "Lily, be sensible. There's guards all over."

"Just come on," she said.

Henry was about to go after her when he saw a gold cross on a chain partially embedded in the wall. He dug it out and pulled on the chain. It was stuck. He pulled harder, jumping back in shock as a body in a black cassock fell out from a shallow catacomb-like grave.

"Reverend Michael?" Henry asked, when he had found his voice again.

Lily nodded, still trying to catch her breath.

Henry frowned, thinking. "Lily, how long ago did Reverend Michael disappear?"

"Just before the change," she said.

That wasn't what he meant, so he shook his head. "No. *Exactly* when?"

"The fall?" Lily guessed.

"And when did the new Reverend come?" Henry asked.

She tried to remember. "After two days, maybe three."

Henry nodded grimly, having expected that. "He's a fraud, Lily. They could never have gotten somebody here that quickly. It takes that long just to get word to the States."

They looked at each other, knowing that Reverend Drury must be a very dangerous man, and that they were in very deep trouble.

"Come on," Henry said. He started down the tunnel.

They moved cautiously, hugging the walls and, after rounding the curve, they saw two boxes of dynamite — with a burly guard sitting on top of them. They pulled back a few feet, watching as the guard stretched out to catch a nap. But he must have heard them moving because he got up and headed towards them to investigate.

As he came around the bend, Henry was ready and clubbed him on the back of the head. The guard didn't even have time to cry out before he slumped to the floor.

"Hurry!" Lily said urgently.

Henry opened one of the boxes of dynamite, wrapped five sticks into a bundle with one fuse and stuffed them into his shirt before backing out the way they had come in.

There was a commotion in a nearby passage and they crept over to see six Indians in chains, guarded by three soldiers carrying rifles. The Indians were the missing warriors from the hunting parties, now being forced to work as slaves, shoveling dirt and pulling carts.

Lily's mouth dropped open. "The hunters!" she breathed.

The tallest and most defiant brave was Matthew, Peter's older brother. He was chained to a cart and the soldiers repeatedly pushed and kicked him to try and make him cooperate.

"Matthew," Lily whispered against Henry's ear. "Peter's big brother."

The Haida workers all turned, apparently hearing someone coming towards them. From their expressions, it was obvious that it was someone who they feared.

The guards pushed the Haidas out of the way, clearing a path, and Henry and Lily took advantage of the diversion to move closer and see what was going on.

Heath, the owner of the general store, stepped into the room and a tall man behind him walked up to Matthew and slapped him. Matthew spit at him and as the man jerked back, Henry and Lily recognized Reverend Drury. The Reverend drew back his arm to slug Matthew and Henry cocked his rifle, taking aim at the phony clergyman.

"Stop, or I'll put a bullet between your eyes!" he yelled.

Reverend Drury laughed and moved towards the sound of Henry's voice. "Is that you, Henry? Congratulations — you're the first to get through."

"Get back!" Henry ordered.

Reverend Drury smiled and halted, only about fifty feet away. "You sound so sinister, Henry. I told you we have the same religion." He paused. *"Gold."*

Lily drew back the arrow in her bow, aching to kill, but Henry shook his head at her. She looked at him, and then relaxed the string, her hands still tensed.

"Who are you, Mister?" Henry asked. "Because I sure know you're not a preacher."

"No," Reverend Drury conceded. "I'm just another greedy American like yourself."

"I'm not like you," Henry said.

Reverend Drury's laugh was patronizing. "Now, Henry. You, if anyone, should understand," he said. "Look at all this gold. The indians aren't miners — they never came up here. Who would it hurt?"

Henry couldn't believe the man's selfish stupidity. "Who?" he asked. "You *starved* these people — and stole from them at the same time."

Reverend Drury shook his head. "This is not the way I planned it. I thought they'd move. But then, Reverend Michael — what can I say? He was a fool."

"Yeah, well, you're sick, Mister," Henry said.

"Harsh words, Henry, very harsh words," Reverend Drury said. Then he smiled. "But I'm not going to let you turn on your own people. I'm prepared to offer you a piece of everything we take out of this mine from here on in. What do you say?"

Henry shook his head. "It's not yours to give."

Reverend Drury took a few steps closer. "Sure it is, Henry."

Henry aimed his rifle at him, his finger quivering against the trigger. "Get back!" he warned. "Or I'll shoot!"

"Do we have a deal?" Reverend Drury asked, moving closer and closer.

Henry couldn't make himself fire, but when he saw the Reverend slip his hand into his cassock, he watched the hand, waiting to see if it would reappear with a Bible — or a gun. When he saw the gun butt, he pulled the trigger, hitting Reverend Drury in the shoulder.

"Get him!" Reverend Drury shouted, clamping his hand to the wound as he dropped to his knees. "Get him!"

As the guards charged, Henry and Lily turned and saw the guard Henry had knocked out was now conscious and blocking their path. There was only one other passageway and they had no choice but to take it.

They ran down the tunnel as fast as they could, slowing only when they saw a dead end about ten yards ahead. They stopped, looking around wildly for something — anything — that would help them escape, hearing the guards getting closer every second.

They were cornered.

Chapter 24

Henry and Lily looked at each other desperately.

"Wait a minute," Henry said. "Listen."

Lily strained her ears. "What?"

"It's White Fang," Henry said, starting to grin. He followed the muffled yelping over to a crevice, sticking his head inside to listen. "Lily, this way!"

Lily ran over and slithered in first, Henry going after her. The space was narrow and claustrophobic, and they struggled to climb up the steep, slippery grade.

Lily slipped and Henry dropped his rifle so he could grab her arm as she slid by. He was able to slow her progress and she got her footing, ready to start climbing again.

Just then, a guard's hand grabbed her ankle and pulled her down further. Lily grabbed Henry's boot, trying to save herself, and he was pulled down with her. Knowing that he would be caught if she didn't let go, she released his boot, allowing herself to be pulled down alone.

"Go on, White Wolf!" she said. "Go on!"

"Lily!" he yelled, as she was pulled into the darkness below. "Lily!" Then, hearing the guards' voices, he forced himself to keep climbing.

Outside, White Fang was digging at the crevice with both paws, widening the hole. Henry pulled himself up and out, setting the salvaged sticks of dynamite on the ground next to him. White Fang wagged his tail and started jumping on his back, but Henry pulled him down, hiding behind some bushes.

A group of guards passed the bushes, searching for him. They went by without seeing him, but Henry still didn't know how they were going to escape. He looked down at the rock wall blocking the canyon, and then looked at the sticks of dyamite.

There was only one way.

Holding the dynamite aloft with his right hand, Henry belly-slid down the wall and into the herd of caribou. He scrambled to his feet and hugged the rocks, barely managing to stay out of the way as the panicky caribou reared up, clashing antlers and hooves as they fought each other for space.

One of the caribou nipped Henry and he wanted to scream, but remembering his lesson from Moses, he settled down, gained control of his fear, and faced the herd of wild animals head on.

"I'm invisible," he told himself. "They can't see me." With a tremendous effort of concentration, he combated the monster of mortality and relaxed, creating a zone of safety around himself.

Up above him, guards were patroling along the edge of the canyon, but they didn't see him walking among the caribou. He strolled calmly through the animals, heading directly for the rock wall.

He was the White Wolf; he was invisible.

Inside the mine entrance, Heath and two guards with rifles watched the hills, waiting for Henry to appear, while Reverend Drury bandaged his arm.

"We're wasting time, Leland," Heath said nervously. "The kid's halfway to Dawson by now to get help."

Reverend Drury frowned at him. "He's got dynamite. He'll blow the wall." Satisfied that the bandage would hold, he pushed his sleeve back down. "Go get the girl."

"Look, let him have the caribou," Heath pleaded. "Starving people, killing — it's enough, already."

"You idiot!" Reverend Drury said, backhanding him across the face. "If the caribou run now, we'll never get down. Get the girl!"

By now Henry had reached the wall and set the dynamite in place. Then he struck a match, which went out in the harsh wind before he could light the fuse.

A guard saw him and fired a wild shot. Quickly, Henry took cover behind a mound of dirt. He was sure that it was all over when he saw White Fang leap at the guard. The man fired another hurried shot, but missed, and before he could discharge the spent shell, White Fang had knocked him down. The guard yelled in terror and ran off.

The second match went out and Henry groaned. He only had one left. He changed position, blocked the wind with his body, and struck the match on his pants. He cupped the flame with both hands, protecting it, then brought it to the fuse, and lit the end.

When the fuse started to fizzle, Henry grinned over at White Fang, but his grin faded when he heard Lily scream. He climbed swiftly up the rocks and looked over the edge of the wall to see Heath and Reverend Drury dragging her out of the tunnel towards a wagon loaded with sacks of gold.

The two men tied Lily inside the wagon. Then Reverend Drury turned in Henry's general direction.

"We're leaving, Henry!" he yelled. "You blow that wall now, you'll kill this girl!"

Lily lunged up and bit his hand, and Reverend Drury slapped her.

Seeing that, Heath lost his temper and

slugged the Reverend, who fell to his knees.

"That's it, Leland," Heath said. "No more. I'm through."

As Heath turned his back to untie Lily, Reverend Drury stood up and clubbed him to the ground with both fists, then kicked him under the wheel of the wagon.

That accomplished, Reverend Drury hopped aboard and whipped the mules with the reins, taking off with Lily and the gold in the back.

Heath rolled clear of the wheels at the last second, kicking at them in anger.

While Henry was distracted by all of that, a bullet hit nearby and a rock exploded by his face. He covered his head with one arm, his mind on the dynamite burning below. He was going to have to put it out.

Reaching down, his hand slipped. The bundle was knocked down between some of the rocks. Henry jammed his arm between the boulders, but the dynamite was still inches from his fingertips.

He knew he had to make a decision, but his mind was a total blank. Hearing a hollow clucking sound, he looked around and saw the raven in a tree.

The raven bobbed his head up and down, and from side to side, clucking and clucking. Then it flew away, with White Fang hot on its trail, leaping out of the canyon and up the hill.

Henry looked at the burning fuse on the dynamite and then followed White Fang, who was still following the raven. Bullets landed all around as Henry dashed out of the canyon and up the steep hillside.

Suddenly the wall exploded with a tremendous BOOM!, opening a huge hole. The terrified caribou froze, staring at their freedom.

Up on the hill, Henry ran hard, not knowing where they were going, following the Wolf who followed the raven. They ran farther and farther, up and up, into the dark forest. Henry stumbled, and when he looked up, he couldn't see White Fang anywhere.

"White Wolf!" a familiar voice yelled.

Henry saw Peter at the top of the hill, waving him on before running away.

Henry waved back and started climbing.

"Peter!" he called. "Peter, wait!"

He caught up to his friend and they ran side by side, Peter pushing him on.

"Where we going?" Henry gasped.

Peter just raced ahead, chasing after the wolf. Henry followed them up the steep ground to the top where he ran around the same bend from his dream and stopped next to White Fang at the edge of the cliff and the raven flew away over the pass.

Henry looked around, wondering where Peter had gone. His friend had disappeared, as if into thin air. Below them, he could see the wagon rumbling along with the Reverend and Lily inside.

Drury was getting away!

Back at the hole in the wall, the caribou moved slowly at first, but once they tasted freedom, it turned into an all-out stampede. The crazed caribou poured through the opening, fighting for position, the power of nature unleashed.

God help anything or anyone that got in their way.

On the cliff above the pass, Henry crouched low, his arm around White Fang's neck, ready to leap off. He felt the wolf's muscles tense as they both waited, poised, one and the same.

"You and me, boy," Henry said.

Feeling the wolf rock back before he jumped, Henry did the same and blindly followed the wolf right off the cliff.

Chapter 25

Something caught Reverend Drury's eye as he drove the mules, using the whip viciously, and he looked up. His mouth fell open as he saw White Fang and Henry, side by side, leaping from the cliff.

They sailed through the air and landed in the back of the wagon near Lily. White Fang recovered his balance first and slammed into Reverend Drury's chest, knocking both of them over the side.

Reverend Drury landed on White Fang with all of his weight before grabbing a tree root to stop his headlong fall down the hill. White Fang kept rolling, injured, down to the bottom, where he lay still.

Reverend Drury swore, and started climbing back up to the road to go after his gold.

Slamming around in the back of the out-of-control wagon, Henry untied Lily and they jumped to safety as the mules went one way and the wagon — flipping its gold into the air — went over the side of the hill.

Reverend Drury ran to the spilled sacks. "My gold! My gold!"

Henry and Lily heard the thunder of the hooves and ran off the pass as the wild herd of caribou came stampeding over the rise. They ducked down, trying to stay out of the way.

When Reverend Drury saw that the herd was headed straight for him, he dropped his gold and tried to run. But he tripped on the hem of his cassock and fell to the ground, screaming in horror.

The herd of caribou trampled the Reverend, then pounded out of the forest and into the tall grass.

In the sudden silence, Henry and Lily saw White Fang still lying in a crumpled heap and slid down to him.

"White Fang!" Henry cried, and bent to

check his injuries as White Fang struggled to get up. "Be still, boy. You have to be still."

He picked up the injured wolf in his arms and with Lily behind him, they walked into the forest and headed back to the village.

When they got there, after passing through a field of peacefully feeding caribou, Moses and Kat'rin were waiting for them. Moses lifted the wolf from Henry and laid him down where Kat'rin could care for him. Then he took Henry and Lily into his arms and hugged them, with tears bright in his eyes.

"Moses," Henry said, not sure where to start.

"It is done now," Moses said.

Henry nodded. There was nothing more to say.

Moses turned and looked at his niece sadly, which was when Henry noticed Peter's dead body lying on the ground. He stared at the limp form, shocked.

"They couldn't catch him," Moses said. "So they shot him in the back."

Henry stared at Peter, unable to believe it, in spite of the horrible evidence in front of his eyes.

"No, that's impossible," he said. "I was just running with him. He was right beside me."

Moses and Kat'rin smiled magically, enjoying the thought.

"Peter loved to run," Kat'rin said in a fond voice, and Moses nodded.

Henry waited for more, but there was nothing.

Moses smiled at something behind him and Henry saw Matthew and the other lost Haida hunters leave the forest. Moses hugged Matthew — his remaining son — tightly, as thankful to see him as he was unhappy to have lost Peter.

Henry just looked at his fallen friends — Peter, dead; White Fang, badly injured.

How come *he* had made it through unscathed?

They took White Fang to the Wolf House, where Lily and Kat'rin cleaned his wounds. Henry crouched nearby, stroking the wolf's head to comfort him.

"I won't let him die," Lily promised.

Henry nodded. White Fang lifted his head enough to lick Henry's hand and then fell back weakly.

Moses and the rest of the villagers were watching silently behind them, and when Moses started a healing chant, they all joined in.

Henry mouthed the words, too, praying for his friend's recovery.

He spent the night sitting by the fire with Moses and Matthew, watching White Fang sleep.

Seeing how tired he was, Lily crept out of her blankets.

"Sleep," she said softly. "I will watch him."

Feeling secure with her there, Henry curled up on his side, listening to her sing her healing song. This time, it was for the wolf.

He soon fell asleep. In the morning he awoke to the din of a raven's cackle. Finding himself alone in the room, he went outside.

Lily was sitting by the river and she pointed at White Fang, who was lying by the water's edge, looking much stronger. Cinnamon was right beside him, and she rested her paw on his back.

Henry laughed and looked at Lily, whispering "Thank you." She shrugged, shyly.

A noisy raven swooped down out of no-where and landed on the bank nearby. He cocked his head and looked at them strangely, clucking away.

"Peter," Henry said, and Lily smiled in agreement. "Just like he promised."

Then the raven flew off.

Once they had been left alone, a guilty sadness shaded Lily's expression and she got up and walked into the woods.

Realizing that she was really leaving, Henry chased after her.

"Lily, stop!" he said. "What's wrong?!"

She led Henry to her secret place, dropped down, and dug in the soft earth, using her knife as a shovel.

Confused, Henry knelt down and helped her dig. She struck a board, cleared off the remaining dirt, and lifted it up. Underneath it was the gold-filled pack that Henry had lost in the rapids.

"You found it," Henry said, stunned. He opened the pack, seeing all of his gold sacks safely inside.

"White Fang is well enough to travel," Lily said. "Now you can go."

"But . . ." Henry blinked, confused. "I don't want to go."

"Please," she said. "Just leave." And she ran off.

Henry started to go after her, but then stopped, realizing the hopelessness of their situation. He sank down onto a nearby stump and stared at all of the hard-earned gold spread out at his feet.

Instead of being happy, he felt utterly lost and alone. Gold no longer meant anything to him, but *Lily* did.

Chapter 26

When Lily didn't return, he gave up and trudged back to the village. He gathered his belongings and started packing his mule, his mood somber as he prepared to leave.

"Where will you go now?" Moses asked.

Henry shook his head, fastening the straps on one of the mule's baskets. "I don't know yet."

"Where is home?" Moses asked.

That was a question to which Henry no longer knew the answer.

"San Francisco," he said, "but there's nothing for me there. Not anymore."

Moses looked surprised. "Nothing? Not even for a man with gold?"

"Nothing I'm interested in," Henry said glumly. "Nothing I want."

Moses nodded, knowing that he was speaking about Lily. "Come back in the spring," he said.

Henry suddenly looked vulnerable and uncertain. "That's a long way off. Maybe . . . I mean . . ." He stopped. "If you see Lily . . ."

Moses nodded, and then moved his jaw. "Something I didn't tell you about Haida women."

"What's that?" Henry asked, even though it didn't really matter anymore, now that Lily had rejected him.

Moses grinned wryly. "You never know what they will do. It's one of the secrets of their strength." His grin got even more crooked. "Sometimes they even surprise themselves."

"Well." Henry forced a smile. "I'll try to remember that." He looked at the older man with deep gratitude, and then embraced him. "Thank you, Moses — for everything."

"You were the one who did the giving," Moses said. He clasped a strong hand on Henry's shoulder. "May the Great Spirit and all the spirits keep you and protect you, White Wolf. You are a person of courage and of honor. When we speak of you, it will be with pride."

Now Kat'rin came over and hugged Henry, too.

"Be happy, White Wolf," she said. "We'll keep you in our hearts."

"And I'll do the same," Henry promised. "But I'm still going to miss you, all of you."

As he turned to mount up, he realized that all the members of the village, including Matthew and the lost hunters, had gathered at the perimeter to wish him farewell — all of them, that is, except Lily.

"Good-bye!" Henry said, receiving their shouted "Good-byes" in return.

Then he nudged the mule lightly and began to ride out of the village towards whatever lay in his future.

White Fang saw him departing and, after one last nuzzle with Cinnamon, ran to join him, leaving the she-wolf behind.

They were right back where they had started, before the raft capsized — on their way to Dawson, with thirty sacks of gold.

Lily stood indecisively in the forest, holding something that she put under her arm. Then she dashed through the woods towards the village as if she were running for her life. She made her way through the villagers standing by the Wolf House as Henry and White Fang were just about to disappear around a bend in the path.

"White Wolf!" she called out as loudly as she could.

Henry stopped, looking back.

Lily stood in the middle of the village and put on the shawl Henry had given her. She had skillfully woven shells, feathers, and leather fringe into it — the marriage of two cultures.

For a moment, all was very still and Henry waited right where he was, speechless.

Lily took a deep breath, summoning all her courage. "White Wolf — I choose you," she said.

He ran to her, and they came together, holding each other tightly as the village erupted in cheers of approval.

"Lily!" Henry said, almost beside himself.

"I choose you, Henry Casey," Lily answered, her voice choked with emotion.

Then they kissed.

As White Fang happily stared up at the two lovers, and waved his tail, Cinnamon came out of the forest. She and White Fang shared a long look and then the two wolves ran to each other. If wolves had human expressions, theirs would have said, "At last!"

It was two months later and Henry and Lily were running through the forest behind White Fang. The wolf entered a den hidden under the exposed roots of a huge tree, and Henry and Lily scampered up the hill after him, crawling in, too.

Inside lay White Fang and Cinnamon, and their four new cubs. Three of them were cinnamon girls and the other was a gray and white male who looked just like White Fang.

Henry picked up Little White Fang gently, and Cinnamon licked his hand as the cub wriggled in his palm. Henry stared at the tiny cub, fascinated.

"Breathe in his nose," Lily said. "Let him know it's you."

Henry put the cub's nose to his open mouth and breathed into it. To his amazement, the cub responded noticeably and nuzzled his fingers, oddly familiar with him.

As Lily smiled, Henry put the cub down beside Cinnamon. Little White Fang burrowed between two of the cinnamon cubs and began to suckle, already the dominant male.

Henry patted White Fang's head, and then took Lily's hand in his, all of them lying comfortably together in the small, warm den.

Man, Woman, and Wolves had all become one big, happy family.